Shrewsbury Station Just After Six

Philip Gillam

Copyright © 2013 Philip Gillam

All rights reserved.

ISBN: 1484933397
ISBN- 13 978-1484933398

For my darling wife Carol and our three wonderful sons,
Dave, Tom and Alex, with all my love.

CONTENTS

	Acknowledgments	i
1	Vicky's Little Garden Party	1
2	A Bright Golden Haze On The Meadow	14
3	Unavoidable Yearnings	28
4	Penny And Alastair In October	41
5	Backhoe Billy, Back-Again Beth	53
6	Happiest Of Moments	64
7	A Little Friend To Play With	78
8	Triumph At The Village Hall	90
9	Shrewsbury Station	100
10	The Belle Vue Tavern	113

ACKNOWLEDGMENTS

A special thank you to Laura Davey for the cover illustration. And to David Gillam for the cover design. Thanks also to Jan and Betty and Dave for their support, feedback and suggestions. And thanks also to Mansel and Clare and the good people of Belle Vue for their inspiration. Special thanks also to singer-songwriter Brian Crane for permission to use his lyrics.

CHAPTER ONE

VICKY'S LITTLE GARDEN PARTY

A wasp zig-zagged and bumped repeatedly against the outside of the patio window. The distant hum of a lawnmower was the only interruption to the intoxicating peace. The softest of breezes nudged at the flowers. Everything looked perfect and lush.

It was a warm and pleasant evening in August and twenty-three-year-old Vicky Clayton was lighting large candles in the garden in preparation for a small party with half a dozen of her friends. It was almost seven o'clock, but, with the weather being so fine, there was still the prospect of plenty more daylight to be enjoyed.

Sitting in a shaded area near the shed was the family's cat, a well-loved creature with a smooth coat of ginger and white. Vicky smiled at the animal and said: "Is this a shocking waste of good candles, Chesterton? I mean they're scented ones as well. Scented candles in a garden?" But her feline companion was unmoved by the question. "You see the thing is, my furry friend, it won't be dark for ages. It's not like we're in need of illumination, is it?" Again the cat showed no interest. "Oh, what the heck!" Vicky said. "Let's live a little! You can't beat a few nice scented candles to cheer the place up."

Her friends were due to arrive soon. She surveyed the garden one last time to make sure she was satisfied with its appearance. She had taken all the washing in off the line so that the place looked its best. Vicky noticed – and appreciated not for the first time that day – the rich colours of her mother's magnificent displays of roses, begonias, fuchsias, geraniums and fabulous tumbling lobelia. The glory of the garden made her think of her mum just as, earlier that day, putting all the empty pear cider bottles out for recycling had made her think of her dad.

Looking up, she saw an aircraft, no bigger than a dot. The plane was climbing, climbing, painting a vapour trail of silver against the bright blue of the early evening sky.

The doorbell rang.

"Here they are," she said, this time not even pretending to talk to the cat.

Catching her reflection in the patio window, she hoped she would not look too plain matched against some of her more beautiful friends. "Hey! Check me out?" she said. And spent a moment doing just that. Platinum blonde hair looking good. Pretty pale blue dress. Eye-catching necklace. Not bad, she thought. Not bad at all.

She had resigned herself to being the only "single" person there, all three of her best pals having steady boyfriends at their sides. Vicky had broken up with her last boyfriend – a JCB digger operator from the other side of town – more than a year ago and had not dated anyone since.

"So is this the lot then, Vick?" asked Rachael, the most gorgeous of her friends, as they all took up positions around the large garden table.

Vicky surveyed the scene: three girls, three boys, and herself – oh, and the cat of course. "Well, I did put out invitations to a few others . . . Richard, Jenny, Lizzie Tyler . . . but I'd be very surprised if any of them turn up. So, yeah, it's probably just you guys and me. Can I get you all a drink?"

"Actually, Vick, I *did* take the liberty of asking my brother along too. He's at a bit of a loose end at the moment. Hope you don't mind." It was Zoe Preston who had lit this beacon of hope for the party's hostess.

Vicky was about to say "the more the merrier" when there was another ring of the doorbell.

Connor Preston was decidedly skinny and his hair was a mess, but he had a warm smile and came bearing a small bouquet, and even as Vicky said "Please, come on in and join the party," she knew she was going to like him.

"Love this house," he told her as she led him through to the garden. "Shrewsbury has so many lovely houses, doesn't it?"

Her home – well, her parents' home to be more exact – was a substantial late-nineteenth century house of red brick in a quiet street called South Hermitage in the suburb of Belle Vue. The area had sprung up in dribs and drabs mostly between the 1830s and the 1880s, plot by plot, little by little, reflecting the styles and ambitions of many different architects, many different builders. It had been a neighbourhood intended to house every strata of Victorian society, and so it was that impressive manor houses emerged just across the road from working class terraces. Shaped by the contours of the railway lines that passed through it, and blessed with a rash of pubs, Belle Vue was not short on charm. In recent decades many of its larger homes had been converted into apartments, but the area remained, by turns, grand then prosaic, aristocratic then plebeian, high-brow yet humble; a lovely district occupying no more than one square mile and the whole enchanting lot being just a brisk walk away from the heart of this proud, historic town.

"So where's your mum and dad?" Connor asked as Vicky presented him with a lager.

"With my grandma for a few days in Lincolnshire."

"Ah. So you've got the place to yourself."

"While the cat's away," said Zoe.

"Well, actually, the cat's *not* away," said Vicky. "You're still here keeping me company, aren't you, Chesterton?" And this time Chesterton did move, heading into the house to find his food.

"This is a bit of a waste, isn't it, Vick?" asked Rachael, gesturing towards the cluster of lighted candles in the middle of the table. "Why don't you wait and light them when it's darker? And what's the point of having *scented* candles when we're sitting in a garden. You should keep the lovely scents for inside."

Before Vicky could reply, Connor said: "Actually, I think they're rather wonderful. They really add something to the gathering. It's very nice that you've taken the trouble, Vicky."

"Well, *you* can come again," said Vicky.

"I wish I'd never mentioned it now," said Rachael with an awkward smile. And the moment passed with no ill feelings.

Vicky had often thought that she would have killed for Rachael's good looks: hair as black as midnight, big dark captivating eyes, voluptuous figure. But for all her beauty, Rachael could often alienate those around her with her knack of putting her foot in it.

As the evening wore on and with three or four lagers inside him, Connor gradually became the centre of attention, telling a few jokes and selecting some unusual CDs to play from Vicky's collection. He became a little louder. More sure of himself. But, thought Vicky, he was nonetheless engaging for his growing confidence.

"Okay we all have to sing along to this track," he said. And sing along they did.

"Vicky, you have a really good voice," he told her.

"Why thank you, kind sir," she said, although she could not quite decide if the compliment was genuine or if it was just the drink talking.

"Tell me something," he said, quietly enough so the others could not hear.

"What?"

"Well, you said earlier that your mum and dad were with your grandma. Does that mean your grandad is no longer around?"

"He died last year."

"I'm sorry to hear that. Were you close?"

"Yeah."

"You miss him?"

"Of course."

"I heard something recently that made me think about life and death. Somebody was talking on the radio and they said that when you look at a gravestone, it isn't the birth date that's important. And it isn't the date of their passing away that's important. What's important is the dash in between."

"I like that," said Vicky. "Let's have another drink."

The evening air cooled and they all went inside, played some more music, talked some more, drank more and nibbled nibbles.

And later, much later, as the party quietened down, Connor again told Vicky: "I really love this house. It's great, isn't it?"

"I know," she said. "I know it's great. And I know you love it because you said so earlier."

"Oh dear. Am I getting boring?"

Vicky gave him a smile which said "Don't be so silly."

Apart from her three years at university, she had lived here all her life, and so, of course, to that extent, it was certainly her home too: not just that of her parents. For Vicky this house was a sanctuary, the comfort of happy memories everywhere. The familiar pictures on the walls, the ornaments, holiday souvenirs like the little ceramic lighthouse in the bathroom, the stacks of books from her childhood still piled high in her bedroom: Harry Potter (because he was never just for boys), The Lion King, Beauty and the Beast, The Little Mermaid – all were precious to her. A pile of old well-read Bliss magazines even now, years after they were last looked at, still nestled up against her collection of well-played-with My Little Pony toys, and then, on the next shelf, The Magic Faraway Tree and other Enid Blyton favourites, and then Spice Girls CDs and an ancient Pick 'n' Mix carton from Woolworths now stuffed full of pencils, pens and highlighters.

Just here in the lounge she was surrounded not only, on this particular evening, by her best friends, but also, this evening and every evening, by pictures and trinkets and souvenirs, any one of which could tell a story.

"Look here," she said, picking up a framed photograph to show Connor. "Mum and dad on one of their very first dates. It's one of their favourite pictures. They were at a seaside fairground. Apparently they'd had the most fantastic day together. They'd persuaded the man who sold the candy floss to take this picture of them. They look so happy, don't they?"

"Why *wouldn't* they be happy? They're obviously in love."

"You're a romantic, aren't you?" she said.

Dodging the subject, he asked what she was drinking. She told him it was pear cider – very sweet, but very nice. "Do you think I could have one?" he asked.

"Of course you can. We have gallons of the stuff. It's funny. When I was at university, pear cider, especially this Swedish stuff, became our drink of choice for a while. One weekend when I was home, I got my dad to try it. He's been hooked on the stuff ever since. Funny because he's really a beer man and this stuff is ever so sweet. But he loves it. Yeah, anyway. I'll get you one."

"Wait. One more question, Vicky, and then I'll come with you to the kitchen and help you find that cider."

"And your question is?"

"Do you love Shrewsbury?"

"Strange question."

"No. Not really. It's just that I love it and I want to know if you feel the same way."

"Oh, definitely," she said. But she was feeling a little sleepy now and did not want to talk too much. And, besides, she was afraid that by saying anything else, she might break the spell she now felt existed between herself and Connor. Oh, yes, she loved Shrewsbury, but how much more mysterious to just leave it at that without going into detail. He would not want to know (would he?) that she loved the quirky names of many of the town's small businesses: cafes and restaurants like

Renaissance and Poppy's and Cromwell's and Mad Jack's; shops like Shoe B Do and Twinkle Twinkle. Of course she was aware that her own love of Shrewsbury was relatively superficial while her parents' passion for the town was deeper, more profound. Her mum and dad were fans of local historians Barrie Trinder and David Trumper. The former wrote heavyweight, painstakingly researched tomes offering forensic detail, whilst the latter produced volumes of sumptuous old photographs of the town and its people, presenting the faces of the long-gone, those smiles and grimaces and expressions of sadness or resignation or surprise; and also the clothes those people wore, men in flat caps or bowler hats, women in extravagant bonnets or the simple dress of housemaids, and also the children – those little girls' pigtails tied up in ribbon.

"I walked here tonight 'cos I fancied a few drinks, but I have a car and I'll pick you up Monday night around seven o'clock." Connor was saying all this to her on the doorstep, but Vicky could not remember having had a conversation about going anywhere on Monday evening.

"Er . . . well, just hang on a minute."

"Oh, sorry. Are you doing something else Monday night?"

"I might be."

"Oh."

"I'll have to check my diary."

"Oh, come off it, Vicky!" It was Rachael who had crept up behind her in the hallway. You don't even have a diary. You told me that the other day. You don't have a diary because if you had one you'd have nothing to put in it."

"Oh, well, thanks a lot for that, Rachael. I don't think Connor really needs to know that, somehow. Yes, yes. You're quite right of course. I have no social life and I'm destined to die alone in a creepy old house full of cobwebs. But that's not necessarily something I wish the whole world to know."

"Oops! Sorry Vick." And, with that, Rachael – her boyfriend suddenly in tow – slipped past the two of them, said goodnight with a sheepish smile, and was gone.

Vicky took a deep breath.

"And so Connor. I'm not entirely sure where all this is leading, but, yeah, I am free on Monday night."

"Excellent."

"So what were you saying?"

"I'll pick you up at seven-ish?"

"I'll look forward to it."

"Good. You do have a lovely singing voice, you know?"

"Er, thanks. That's twice now you've told me that. So where are we going Monday night?"

"Surprise!"

"Mmmmmm."

"But I'll tell you this much, Vicky Clayton. I promise you an evening to remember. Perhaps even an evening that will change your life."

"That's quite a claim, young man."

"Well, maybe it is."

"There's no 'maybe' about it."

"Well, I like to keep a girl guessing." And, with that, he walked out onto the street, waving and smiling like an idiot.

The following evening,
the market town of Louth, Lincolnshire

"Do you want one, Alastair?" His mother-in-law's call from the kitchen meant that she had put the kettle on yet again. Just how many cups of tea, he wondered, could a man drink in one day before exploding.

"Oh, go on then," he shouted back from his privileged position in the lounge, the television providing undemanding entertainment before him, the Sunday Times stretched out on his lap.

Even with the TV on, he could still just make out not the words but the rhythms of the chatter coming from the other room, the short sharp bursts of conversation, those oh so

Shrewsbury Station Just After Six

familiar patterns of speech between his wife and her mother – the Denby girls as he liked to call them.

Five minutes later the tea arrived in a mug that had been around a good few years, a mug that – in its time – had doubtless seen every room in this old house; that had sat on a bedside table on many a morning offering the first cuppa of the day or had rested on a step ladder during painting and decorating sessions. It was a mug that had been down the garden countless times, perhaps perched on an outcrop of rockery next to flower beds or else surrounded by tomato plants in the greenhouse with the once vibrant, now recently deceased Mr Denby. He was the man who had been the senior horticulturalist of this family, Olivia's much-missed husband, Penny's much-missed dad. Surely it had been her dad who had given Penny her own talent for gardening.

Alastair looked up. "Thanks Olivia," he said. "Oh, and biscuits as well. You're too good to me. Anyway, when are you going to release my darling wife from her servitude and allow her and your good self to come and sit down in here and watch a bit of telly?"

"Oh, we won't be long now. We've finished all out chores. She's just helping me sort out some knitting. We're working together on the kitchen table. We're perfectly happy." And then she was gone again, leaving Alastair with his mug of tea, the newspaper and Antiques Roadshow.

He looked idly around the room, deciding after all that he didn't especially want his umpteenth hot drink of the day, that the contents of his newspaper were actually rather dull, and that he had no particular interest in the antiques being discussed by Fiona Bruce and a fierce-looking woman from Edinburgh.

He switched off the television and looked out of the bay window at the tired, neglected street of between-the-wars housing.

Considering his immediate situation, Alastair now ran his fingers through his grey hair and took stock of his unwanted tea going cold, the scattered broadsheet pages, the sweetly

9

depressing scene beyond the window, the prospect of more inconsequential Sunday night television.

"Oh dear," he said to himself.

So what would his idea of paradise be right now? A decent hi-fi turned up loud for a start. Maybe sipping ice cold Kopparberg Swedish pear cider whilst looking out upon rolling countryside with snow-capped mountains in the distance?

He heard his wife laughing in the kitchen and he smiled.

They had met twenty-seven years earlier and their first date had been, unimaginatively enough, an evening at the cinema. Alastair couldn't even remember now the film they had been to see. Their second date, three days later and a thousand times more memorable, was at a fairground in Skegness where they had been giggly in the August sun, where they had been silly like school pals on holiday together, where they had allowed themselves to be children again for a few hours; a ride on the ghost train, getting all sticky with candy floss, sharing a car on the dodgems.

A boisterous, unpredictable breeze would, from time to time, disperse the deep warmth of that summer's afternoon. It was a breeze that carried with it the aroma of cheap hamburgers sizzling in the serving hatches of dazzlingly decorated vans.

As the two of them dawdled around between the rides, thumping pop music fused in the air with the laughter of over-excited children.

Most memorable of all, Alastair now reflected, were the brightly painted swings, those big wooden swings in which two people can sit facing one another. There were several sets of them in a far corner of the fairground. A father and son were sitting in one. A mother and daughter in another. But several were occupied by young couples.

Alastair and Penny climbed aboard a swing of primrose yellow and as they glided to and fro in this magic sun-soaked chariot, they talked and talked like they needed to get it all out before the swinging stopped. They quickly found they had nothing in common but rather than being discouraged by this, they revelled in their lack of similarity, laughing affectionately at each other's likes and dislikes.

Alastair told her he loved Woody Allen films. "The man's a comic genius," he enthused. "So insightful, don't you think?"

"To be honest, I just find him creepy," she said. "Sorry, but I do."

They stared at each other for a moment.

And then they roared like they were being tickled by God.

"What? Are you mad? Are you crazy? How can you not like Woody Allen? Okay. Okay. Okay. What about music?" he asked.

She loved The Carpenters and Art Garfunkel. He was into folk-rock singer-songwriters like Donovan and Cat Stevens and Nick Drake.

She liked romantic novels, he loved science fiction.

She loved Italian food, he loved egg and chips.

And yet . . .

And yet . . .

He heard his wife's voice. She was still in the kitchen, still talking with her mother. "Have you got a cable needle?"

Her mother didn't hear her daughter's question because, doubtless, she was too busy concentrating on something else. They never stop being busy, these Denby girls, Alastair thought, picking up a biscuit and then putting it back down on the plate.

Penny continued thinking aloud: "So that's seven. Pattern. Four across. Pattern. Thirty-nine. One, two, three, four. . . . Have you got a little cable needle, Mum? I don't know if I've got the right-sized needle here."

Olivia said something in reply, but Alastair didn't catch it.

Then Penny was counting again: "Thirty-two, thirty-three, thirty-four, thirty-five . . . Oh, that's interesting. Cast off seven stitches."

There was a pause and then Olivia asked: "Do you think that's where I've gone wrong?"

Listening to the two of them from his armchair in the lounge, Alastair laughed out loud. He would not have been able to explain why.

He was eavesdropping on his wife and his mother-in-law, a cold mug of tea beside him. Yet he was laughing as he had laughed all those years ago on that fairground's painted swing.

And then the phone rang. Olivia got there first. "Hello."

"Oh, hi Grandma. It's Vicky."

"Hello Sweetheart. How are you?"

They chatted for a few moments about the weather in Lincolnshire compared to the weather in Shropshire and about the latest episode of a TV soap they both followed. And Vicky told Olivia that she had had a very quiet day indeed; a long lie-in followed largely by sitting around in her dressing gown, watching trashy telly and eating chocolate.

"Sounds like heaven," her grandma said. "Anyway, Sweetheart. I'll pass you on to your mum."

"Hi Vick. How did your little garden party go last night? You haven't trashed the place, I trust."

"As if," said Vicky. "We just played a few CDs, we talked for hours. Yeah, and we drank quite a lot."

"Got a hangover?"

"No. Not really."

Alastair was listening in to the conversation and smiled at the idea of his daughter's garden party with her friends. He recognised in himself a small yearning to break away from his middle-aged life and be young again, a little desire to actually have been there at that garden party, playing CDs and drinking too much. He also knew that to have attended his daughter's get-together would have been to invite ridicule like some geriatric at a rave.

A year ago, Vicky and a couple of friends had attended the Reading Festival, sharing a small tent and having the time of their lives. And although Alastair had never had any great love of camping, he fantasised about going with a couple of his mates to Reading or Glastonbury one year. He hated the idea that he was too old to do it.

The more he thought about it now, the stronger the notion grew. Yes, it was not just some passing fancy. He wanted to don a younger man's clothes, adopt a younger man's attitude, even if he could never reupholster his skeleton in a younger man's skin. He wanted to be able to stand with a crowd in a field, watching a band whose thunderous power chords could shake mountains. He wanted to be with a group of mates. He wanted to be able to laugh enough, and to listen to music enough and to down alcohol enough, if that's what it took, so that he might glimpse the deep untouchable mysteries of life. Oh, to soak up the stuff of the gods, the stuff that was so surely there, just there, just out of reach – beyond the here and now.

"So who was actually *there* at this party then, Vick?" asked Penny.

"Oh, Rachael and Joe, Amy and Steve, Zoe and James."

"Oh dear. So you were a Billy-no-mates in the midst of three couples?"

"Thanks for pointing that out, Mum."

Vicky had decided not to mention Connor, and she certainly did not wish to tell her parents that in less than twenty-four hours she would be embarking upon her first date in more than a year, her first date since breaking up with the JCB digger operator from the other side of town. She had no wish to mention she would be going she knew not where, with a young man she knew barely at all – nor that he had promised her a night to remember, perhaps even one that would change her life. If she had even hinted at any of this, her mum and dad would have – *would have what?* First, teased her mercilessly. And then have worried that she might be about to be kidnapped by a pervert. And Vicky did not want them to become anxious when they should be having a relaxing time with her grandma.

"I'm not quite an old maid yet, Mum," she said.

"Sorry Darling. I didn't mean . . . "

"It's okay, Mum. You're still invited to the wedding should I stumble upon Mr Right."

CHAPTER TWO

A BRIGHT GOLDEN HAZE ON THE MEADOW

*Nestled in the horseshoe
of a winding river's course
Standing proud upon a hill
Is the old town of my youth.
With towering church spires
And ramparts of rugged stone.
It's seen the harvest gathered in
And felt the anger of the sword*

(from the song 'Old Town' by Brian Crane)

Alastair was already looking forward to going back to Shrewsbury. The lion's share of the second week of his fortnight's holiday beckoned and he would spend it in his beloved home town. He had no problem with Louth and he could happily spend a few days there, but he was never more contented than when he was at home. Of course he also knew that when the moment came to leave Lincolnshire and to leave Olivia in her quiet and husbandless house, his wife and his mother-in-law would shed a few tears, and those hugs and farewells would herald another highly emotional wrench for the Denby girls as they parted company once more. Had he ever had *that* kind of closeness with his own mum and dad, he wondered. No. Probably not. Their passing had been a great sadness to him, but nothing on the scale felt by Penny when her dad had died, and this love between Penny and Olivia was something he almost envied.

It had been a career opportunity back in 1982 which had brought Alastair eastwards to Lincolnshire. Within months he and Penny had met and fallen in love. One year later, another career opportunity arose back in Shrewsbury and the couple married in Louth and then immediately moved to Shropshire to set up home. In the excitement of the moment neither Alastair nor Penny had given a great deal of thought to how the bride's parents may have felt about their only child being taken away to the other side of the country. Visits back and forth over the years would be frequent, but the 125 miles between the two towns would often feel like a much greater distance, especially for the two Denby girls.

At the kitchen table, while waiting for his wife to come down from the bathroom and join him for breakfast, he watched Olivia standing at the sink. They had smiled brightly enough at one another and had talked about the squirrels in the garden that ran up the bird table to steal the food, and about a George Clooney film they had all watched together on DVD the previous evening, and about the headlines in the Daily Mail. But he could tell her smile was forced, that her chatter was a distraction from her true feelings. Alastair knew that as she washed and squashed a milk carton ready for recycling, her mind was already swimming with the reality that twenty-four hours from now her precious daughter would be heading back to Shropshire; that they would not see each other again for weeks, maybe months – nothing had yet been arranged in terms of future visits. Alastair could tell that the dull pain of loneliness was already returning to her, and he felt helpless for not being able to say the right thing now to comfort her, not being able to pluck from the air the words that would make it better for her.

The three of them, Alastair, Penny and Olivia, spent the rest of the morning pottering about in the garden, cutting the lawns, trimming the edges, a spot of weeding and watering, and the whole enterprise accompanied by plenty of tea-drinking and friendly small-talk.

"We'll perhaps watch a nice film tonight, shall we?" asked Olivia. "That George Clooney one was all right, but I fancy something a bit more upbeat if you know what I mean."

"Yeah," said Alastair, praying silently that it would not be one of Olivia's Hollywood musicals. She had them all on DVD. He had never enjoyed them, finding the songs painfully contrived and the performances just daft. He considered these films to be museum pieces, dusty and worn-out, and somehow faintly depressing.

In the afternoon they wandered around the shops in Louth. The Denby girls stocked up on 'smellies'. Alastair treated himself to a book about Donovan, the singer-songwriter who had enjoyed hits in the sixties with Mellow Yellow and Sunshine Superman. Penny would sometimes tease her husband about his enthusiasm for folk-rock, but he was happy to take the gentle joshing.

After the shopping, they found themselves what they had all agreed was "a nice little pub" for an early evening meal.

As the waitress handed out the meals, Olivia asked her son-in-law: "So anyway, Alastair, how's the job going?" Over the previous few days, they had touched on just about every other subject so it was inevitable that the "job question" would arise at some point.

"Oh. You know, Olivia. Same old, same old." Alastair was an estate agent with Penfold, Carroll and Walsh. He would never have said that he loved what he did for a living, but he certainly did not dislike it either.

Olivia and Penny gave each other a knowing look as if to say: "*Same old, same old?* – Well, that's the end of that scintillating conversation, then."

But the question *had* evoked a memory for Alastair, an incident he was not keen to share with his wife and mother-in-law. He had not given much thought to his work or goings-on in the office for several days. After all, he was on holiday and did not wish to think about such things. But now he found himself silently – and secretly – reliving a conversation, leaving Penny and Olivia to tuck into their meals.

Just over a week ago, one of the newcomers to the office, an eye-catching woman called Beth, had waltzed up to his desk and said: "Hey, Al." (Nobody ever called him Al, not even his wife). "We're off to the pub for a quick drink after work. Coming with us?" He was not used to people being so brazen. This woman hardly knew him and was addressing him as "Al". Who did she think she was? But she was attractive and clearly meant no offence so Alastair had nervously doodled something meaningless in his notebook and said: "Er . . . yeah, okay."

Beth was a few years younger than Alastair and, as he thought about her now – as he enjoyed his fish, chips and mushy peas in a little pub in Louth – he considered her to have far more confidence and far more "spirit" than he had *ever* had. Beth was what Alastair's long-dead father might have called "a right little cracker". Or what Alastair's long-dead mother might have called "trouble".

Enjoying a drink with her and a handful of colleagues after work that day, he had found himself captivated by her effervescence and her untainted child-like brightness and optimism; and there was something else too – he could not shake off the notion that she had been flirting with him.

There had been that one moment in particular when she had returned from the bar with drinks and crisps for herself and a couple of others and had turned to him and – flashing her big brown eyes at him – had asked: "So Al. How do you like to spend your evenings?"

Oh, but he was being silly. Why would a lovely woman like that be remotely interested in him?

"How's your fish, Darling?" asked Penny.

"Oh, it's . . . it's absolutely fine. Really. Absolutely fine."

o o o o o o

Fresh from her bath, Vicky has given herself more than enough time to get ready. She sets out her choice of perfumes on the dressing table before her, five bottles, five subtly different scents, three of them Christmas presents, the others birthday gifts.

She sprays a little of the one her mum got her last year: it's light and vivacious. She breathes it in slowly – it is zingy and fruity and somehow suggests the sort of non-committal fun that exists in that space between innocence and naughtiness – and she smiles, and she thinks that this might just be the one for tonight.

She surveys her array of cosmetics and other "products" for lips, eyes, hair, skin, nails. She takes a swig from her chilled Pepsi, rolls a mouthful around on her tongue before swallowing. The coldness and the sweetness and the fizziness of the liquid is good. Wearing only her white fluffy bathrobe, she sits comfortably and relaxed in front of her mirror, and then leans across to her iPod in its dock.

The device is on shuffle and it plays Kings of Leon – 'Knocked Up'. "Whoa, whoa, whoa, whoa, whoa," she says. "Nobody's going to get knocked up tonight. What? Making babies on our first date? I don't think so. No, no, no, no, no. All in good time. All in good time."

She moves the iPod along to the next song, something by Razorlight, all jingle-jangle guitars and shimmering cymbals, something slower and more melodic. It seems to suit Vicky's mood. The music fills the perfumed air. She has not felt this way for some time. What's the word? Ah, yes – happy. That's the word.

Laid out on her bed behind her is a primrose yellow summer dress. It's fresh. Feminine. Pretty as a picture. She reckons that will do the trick.

Taking another swig from her Pepsi, she sets about making

herself beautiful. The My Little Pony figures of her childhood look down from her shelves as Razorlight play on.

o o o o o o

"Now, this is a nasty junction, this one, Alastair, so just be careful." Mother-in-law was in full flight as back-seat driver.

"What on earth are we listening to, by the way?". Penny was in full flight as music critic.

"Oh, this is a singer-songwriter called Brian Crane. He's a Shrewsbury bloke and this song we're listening to right now is actually about Shrewsbury . . . *standing proud upon a hill is the town of my youth*. When me and my mates were nineteen, twenty, twenty-one, something like that, we used to go and see Brian and his band, Paper Bubble, who would play gigs at places like the Lion Hotel. They were folk-rock and they even released an album. They were briefly quite big . . . well, quite big in Shrewsbury anyway. I love this stuff. What's the matter with you? Don't you like it?"

"Paper Bubble? I mean – honestly? Paper Bubble?"

"Yeah okay. Maybe not the greatest name in the world, but that was how it was back then. Iron Butterfly, Plastic Ono Band, Paper Bubble . . . "

"Straw Dogs," offered Penny.

"No. That was a movie, not a band."

And then the back-seat driver added her contribution: "Brass monkeys?"

For the rest of the journey back to Olivia's house the three of them were quiet, but Alastair found that one question now kept playing over and over in his mind, a question which had lain dormant in his tired brain for a week but which had now bubbled to the surface:

"So Al. How do you like to spend your evenings?"

o o o o o o

"You look really nice, by the way," said Connor, taking his

eye off the road for a second to eye her up and down. Shrewsbury was drenched in evening sunlight.

"Well, I didn't have a clue what to wear because you were so secretive about where we were going? Is a dress too much? Would jeans and a top have been better?"

"You're fine," he said.

They were travelling north along the Telford Way and then up past Morrison's on the Whitchurch Road, past what was once the Rolls-Royce engines factory, through the traffic lights at the Harlescott crossroads, past Tesco and through Battlefield. Then the urban landscape gave way to countryside. Trees and hedgerow flashed by.

Vicky scanned the CDs shambolically scattered in the doorwells and in an area at the front of the gearstick. She recognised albums by a number of indie bands including The Killers. She liked The Killers herself. And these albums made perfect sense for a young man like Connor. But there were other CDs in the car which were puzzling – soundtracks to The King and I, The Sound of Music, and South Pacific.

"I didn't have you down as a Rodgers and Hammerstein fan," she said.

"Oh yeah," he said. "I like a bit of variety. You don't want to be listening to the same stuff all the time."

"I guess not . . . So anyway. You still not going to tell me where we're going?"

"And spoil the surprise? Shame on you!"

Connor was wearing smart trousers and a good quality lightweight grey jumper, but Vicky was still worried that she might be just a little overdressed in her primrose yellow summer dress. Was it a pub they were going to? A restaurant? A clue would have been useful.

"Can we listen to this?" she asked, passing him The Killers.

"Sure."

Just after Wem they turned west off the B5476 onto a quiet road flanked by tall hedges so you could not see the fields beyond. This was turning out to be a much longer journey than Vicky had expected. And with each mile travelled, she found the mystery of their destination deepening. It was still daylight, but Vicky, for the first time that evening, began to feel vulnerable. She realised she was a long way from home in a part of the county unfamiliar to her and with a young man she hardly knew at all.

The track called Mr Brightside started up on the CD player.

"I love this one," said Vicky.

"Yeah, me too." said Connor without taking his eye off the road.

Vicky glanced over her shoulder and noticed an impressive-looking camera on the back seat. "Nice camera. What sort is it?" She knew nothing about cameras. She was just making conversation.

"It's a Pentax." he said.

"Oh, right."

He smiled, knowing that she was just being friendly.

But after another few twists in the road, the camera on the back seat began to worry Vicky.

She fleetingly wondered if he was planning to find some remote spot and take what her grandmother would have called "kinky photos" of her. Perhaps her parents had been right to warn her about perverts. "You can't be too careful these days," her mum had told her.

She shook her head: told herself she was just being ridiculous. And she tried to dismiss her nervousness. He seems like such a nice guy, she insisted to herself. He was pleasant, charming, a gentleman. And in the next instant: But what if he likes The Killers not because of their music, but because of their name? And then she was jolted by the song's lyrics about the guy taking off the woman's dress, and Vicky suddenly wondered what she had got herself into.

It was just then that Connor's car faltered and, rolling onwards through the power of nothing but its own momentum, eventually came to a shuddering halt at the side of the road.

"What's going on?" asked Vicky.

Connor looked baffled. "I'm not sure," he said.

"Oh, come off it."

"No really," he said. "I can only think we've run out of petrol."

"What? Nobody runs out of petrol these days. The car warns you these days with little flashing lights and buzzing sounds and electronic messages like *"Watch out! If you're not careful, you'll run out of petrol!"*

Her over-protective father was always telling Vicky not to go off into the countryside with blokes because they'll pretend to run out of petrol and then ravage you in a lay-by. My God, she thought. Dad was right all along. She had always laughed at him, but he was right! Worse than being ravaged in a lay-by, worse than having someone take kinky photos of you with his great big Pentax, worse even than being murdered in a country lane . . . worse than any of this . . . she was going to have to admit to her dad that he had been right all along.

"Hang on," said Connor. He grabbed his mobile from out of his trouser pocket. "Oh, hi there, Jake. Are you at the hall yet?" There was a pause. And then: "Look. I know this sounds completely ridiculous. But I think I must have run out of petrol. Would you mind coming to rescue us? Fill up a can from that petrol station in Wem. That ought to get us back in action. I'll pay you for it. I've got plenty of cash on me. Just forgot to fill up. Cheers, mate. Yeah, yeah. That's it. Okay, okay. Let me tell you where we are . . . "

Fifteen minutes later Jake was there in his Range Rover with enough fuel to get Connor's car going again. Connor and Vicky then followed Jake's vehicle for another five miles until they arrived at the village of Acton Virgil.

Vicky gave Connor a look that said "Now what?" but by now she had at least come to the conclusion that he did not have murder on his mind, and, come to that, not even the notion of ravaging her in a country lane.

They got out of the car and walked across the road and through the main entrance into Acton Virgil Village Hall to be greeted by half a dozen women in long formal dresses from another era, a gathering of men dressed as cowboys, and a small musical ensemble – pianist, flautist, cellist and violinist.

"Okay, people. Let's have another go at 'I Can't Say No'. Sue, are you ready? Musicians, all set, yeah?" The man doing all the shouting was in his fifties and had an air of authority. The woman called Sue took up her position and began singing a song in a ludicrous American accent, a song which improbably managed to rhyme 'pit' with 'forgit'.

"Welcome to The Pigeons," said Connor.

"The what?" asked Vicky.

"Well, we're the Acton Virgil Amateur Operatic Society to give us our full title, but everyone calls us The Pigeons. You see, the village is best known for its famous Acton Virgil Pigeon Fanciers Association. And somewhere along the line the amateur operatic society picked up the nickname of The Pigeons, and we've been stuck with it ever since. Anyway. We're in the middle of rehearsals for Oklahoma!"

"You don't say."

"Oh, don't tell me you know Oklahoma!"

"Yeah. As a matter of fact, I do. My grandma has it on DVD so I've watched it with her a good few times over the years. She loves Rodgers and Hammerstein stuff. Clearly, you love it too, judging by the CDs in your car."

"Well, anyway. I just thought you might like to sit in on a rehearsal tonight. And don't let all the costumes lead you to think, by the way, that we are anywhere near the dress rehearsal stage because we're not. Not by a long way. It's just that several of our members can't resist the urge to dress up. It helps them to get in the mood. Or that's what they say. But it's still early days yet. The show is months away. We're still looking to fill a few of the roles and, as I said the other night, you have a good voice. Thought I might persuade you to join us."

After Sue had finished her number, Connor introduced Vicky to The Pigeons, not missing an opportunity to tell everyone what a 'lovely singing voice' she had.

"If you'd like to try out for us, please do," said the man in his fifties.

Vicky said she would love to have a go and was handed the lyrics to a song called 'Out Of My Dreams'.

"Do you think I might grab a coffee first?"

"Of course. Take five minutes."

Vicky and Connor joined a group of three cowboys in a corner of the hall, chatted for a few minutes about the fun of amateur dramatics, and drank coffee which was much stronger than Vicky was used to, but it did the job.

Then the Shrewsbury girl was ready to take on 'Out Of My Dreams'. The musicians began to play the slow, romantic melody. Vicky knew this song. She loved this song. She and her Lincolnshire grandma had harmonised to it as they had watched the film.

And now she began to sing.

Connor smiled encouragingly. The company gathered around and listened respectfully.

As the song came to a close, the man in his fifties beamed and said: "You know what? That really wasn't bad at all."

And the rest of the cast applauded.

"But it's Laurey Williams who sings this song," said Vicky. "Laurey Williams is the leading lady. Surely, you must have a leading lady."

"We *had* decided who was going to play Laurey Williams," said Connor.

"Yeah, we *had* decided," said one of the women, removing her frilly bonnet as if she were about to pick a fight. "Having already dismissed the idea that *I* might play her because . . . well, because I'm a bit too old for the part . . . Isn't that right, John?"

"Oh, Jane. Don't start all that again, please," said John — the man in his fifties who, Vicky had now decided, was clearly the show's director. "For heaven's sake, do you think Dame Judi Dench is offended nowadays when she isn't offered the part of a young woman contemplating marriage? And, believe me, Jane dearest, I am not for a moment suggesting you are as old as Dame Judi Dench. Anyway, Vicky, yes, we *had* found someone suitable for the role. The fact is, until last week, we had someone very suitable lined up, the right age, the right look, the right kind of voice, the right everything, but she has recently found out that she's having to leave the area because of a promotion at work and so we're a bit stuck on the Laurey Williams front. Or at least we were until tonight. Would you consider it, Vicky?"

"Well, yeah, I would consider it. It's just that . . . "

"What?" asked John.

"Actually, I am already in an amateur dramatics group."

"Well, that wouldn't be a problem for us – would it be a problem for them?"

"I don't think so. I'm not involved in any production with them right now. And, besides, it's not like the West End is it? It's not like I'm in a legally binding contract or anything."

"Who are you with?"

"The Coleham Amateur Theatre Society. The Cats."

"Really? Well, if you join us, Vicky, that'll really put a Cat among the Pigeons."

There were groans all round.

"Well, I promise I won't bite," she said.

On the drive home, Connor asked her if she would like to hear a joke. He did not wait for her reply. "Okay. There's this family of balloons. In the middle of the night the mischievous little boy balloon climbs into his parents' bed. He very carefully unties the little knot on Mummy Balloon and gently lets all the air out. Then he goes over to Daddy Balloon and unties his little knot and lets all the air out. Finally, he unties his own little knot and lets all the air out. In the morning, when Daddy Balloon realises what has happened, he says to the little boy balloon: 'Well, Son. Frankly, you've let me down, you've let your mother down, but, most of all, you've let yourself down'."

Vicky smiled. "That's very sweet."

"Anyway, they seemed to like you at the rehearsal. Are you seriously going to join us?"

"Yes. I think so. Oh, I completely forgot to ask – who's the leading man, by the way? Who's playing Curly?"

Connor turned to her and beamed. "I am. I'm playing Curly. Say hello to your romantic lead."

o o o o o o

Tuesday. The road home from Lincolnshire.

"We're not going to have to listen to Paper Bubble all the way home to Shrewsbury, are we?"

"You can choose what you like, Love. I really don't mind."

He was still enjoying the relief of not having had to endure one of his mother-in-law's blockbuster musicals the previous evening. They had all settled instead for classic clips from Morcambe and Wise.

Penny looked through the CDs in the glove compartment and put on an Art Garfunkel album. She had never tired of Art Garfunkel.

She reached into her bag and gave herself a couple of squirts of Cerruti 1881 which immediately reached her husband's nostrils. He smiled to himself as the floral fragrance filled the car. The smile was not because Penny was wearing perfume, there was nothing unusual about that, but because he suddenly recalled how she – a devoted primary school teacher – would so often come home smelling of poster paints or Plasticine.

She began singing along with the CD and then said: "Of course, being away from home for a few days, you'll have missed out on your cranberry juice and your Omega 3." Penny loved to tease her husband about his health fads.

He ignored her for a few moments, surveying the countryside as he drove. Fields on each side of the road stretched away into the distance. And then he said: "Well, I don't suppose a few days are going to make a lot of difference one way or the other, are they?"

Although, over the recent months, the avalanche of "latest health advice" in the newspapers, proclaiming that "this is good for you" or that "this is bad for you" had left Alastair, for the most part, untouched, he had long ago picked up on reports suggesting that cranberry juice was effective in guarding against urinary tract infections, stomach ulcers, stomach cancer and cardiovascular diseases. He had also read somewhere that

Omega 3 was very good indeed at tackling cholesterol problems and also good for the brain. And so while he was often dismissive of other "health advice" offered in the media, he was utterly convinced that cranberry juice and Omega 3 were nothing short of life-savers.

"I know you think I'm silly, but I honestly believe they're very good for you." he told her as the road took a sudden turn to the right. "Good grief! This sunshine is blinding."

"What's happened to your clip-on sunglasses?" Penny asked.

"Must have left them at home."

"Look at those fields over there. There's a wonderful, yellow haze."

"You'll be bursting into song in a moment. Oklahoma! isn't it? God knows — we've watched it with your mother enough times! Classic Rodgers and Hammerstein, she'd call it. All together now — *There's a bright golden haze on* . . ."

But Alastair's singing trailed off as, taking a sharp turn too quickly, he was momentarily blinded by sunshine. The car slipped away from the road, its chassis scraping against rocks and clumps of earth. It continued out-of-control down an embankment – with Penny screaming "Alastair! Alastair! For God's sake!"

Bumping violently across the rough terrain, the vehicle kept moving. "Aren't the brakes working?" screamed Penny. "Aren't the brakes . . . "

And then the car smashed into a tree with such force that the front of the vehicle crumpled like kitchen foil.

CHAPTER THREE

UNAVOIDABLE YEARNINGS

"Where are you off to, Mum?" Vicky was sitting on the sofa with Connor, the two of them running through their lines for Oklahoma! They each had a glass of pear cider on the go, and – on the small coffee table in front of them – a large bowl of crisps which they were sharing.

Penny grabbed an umbrella from the hallway and called back: "I'm popping up to the hospital first to see your dad, but then I'm off to my Lit and Phil night."

It had been almost four weeks since the accident. Penny had escaped with minor cuts and bruises, but Alastair had suffered not only fractures to his right leg and right arm, but also severe concussion from which he was only now showing signs of a good recovery. Terrible headaches and confusion had given the doctors and his family cause for concern, but the professionals were now saying he was "on the mend" and would be coming home soon. His wife was so relieved by the news that she now felt comfortable with the idea of popping in to see him for just a few minutes, rather than staying the full duration, before heading off to her monthly Literature and

Philosophical Society meeting. The guest speaker was to be a professor from Cheshire who was an expert on Charles Dickens, Penny's favourite novelist.

"I'll come with you to see Dad tomorrow night, if that's okay?" said Vicky. "But, if you don't mind, we really need to get this script cracked."

Penny very nearly called back to them: "Don't you two get up to anything while I'm gone," but then thought better of it. Given that her daughter was a mature twenty-three-year-old, such a comment would have been crass in the extreme. And besides, Penny rather hoped that romance *was* blossoming between them. It would be lovely to have her married and settled – or even unmarried and settled. Penny and Alastair's only child had once had ambition; in terms of love and in terms of career. As a little girl she had dreamed of one day marrying a prince. Well, thought her mother now as she almost tripped over the cat on her way out of the house, there's no harm in dreaming. And on the work front, Vicky – no more than a couple of years ago – had talked of running her own business. She had come away from university with a good degree and had hoped to find work as a fashion designer, but the jobs were simply not there and she had eventually settled for a position as a sales assistant at Next on the nearby retail park. The work did not in any way challenge Vicky, but she enjoyed it well enough and her colleagues had become good mates. She had become comfortable there. Because she had to work most Saturdays, Vicky would often have a day off in the week. And she would very often go into the town centre on such days, relishing the fact that the shops would be quite a bit quieter than on a Saturday. The once-ambitious daughter considered it was not such a bad life.

"I reckon we're almost there now with this script, don't you?" Vicky asked. Connor was wearing the same good-quality lightweight grey jumper he had worn on that first trip to Acton Virgil. She still considered him painfully skinny and thought he could do with "feeding up a bit" as her grandmother would have put it. And his hair was always a mess, but Vicky quite liked it that way.

"Oh, yeah," he said. "It's coming along fine. We're gonna knock 'em dead."

She moved in a little closer to him, sensing this could be a good moment for a celebratory kiss . . . any kind of kiss. It would have been their first. After weeks of seeing each other, weeks of going to rehearsals, weeks of sitting on that sofa together, it would have been their first.

"Anyway," he said. "Looks like your cat wants feeding." And with those words, Connor killed the moment.

Vicky got up from the sofa and Chesterton followed her into the kitchen.

o o o o o o

It was the first Wednesday of September, Vicky's day off. There was a light rain, but not anything that would prevent a young woman from walking down into Coleham, crossing the river by way of the Greyfriars Bridge, and up Wyle Cop into town. The air was fresh and the sun was breaking through intermittently. From the Greyfriars Bridge you could see a rainbow above the church on the bend of the river. Swans were gathering under the bridge in the expectation of breadcrumbs from small children who were being encouraged by mums and dads to throw bits of last week's Hovis into the water.

As she walked up the steep gradient of Wyle Cop, Vicky knew full well that her parents – being such fans of the local historians, Trinder and Trumper – would have been able to wax lyrical about the rich history of the architecture, the fact that Charles Dickens had once stayed at the Lion Hotel, that the stunning black and white buildings to her left included a timber-framed house which was built in about 1460, the time of Richard III for heaven's sake, the king who died at the Battle of Bosworth Field, the decisive battle of the Wars of the Roses; American tourists could only dream of such history back home in the States. For Vicky, though, loving Wyle Cop meant loving the familiarity and the richness of its shops and businesses: Tanners Wine Merchants, The County Sleep Shop, The Period House Shop, the enormous Juliet Chiltern gift emporium, Graphic Heart, the sweet little Wyle Cop newsagents, The Chocolate Gourmet, Oberon women's fashions, The Nag's Head pub, Salopian Sports, the Same Day Dry Cleaners, Bebbington's tearoom, the Severn Hospice shop, the House of Needlework, Snooty Fox – Bespoke Jewellers, and of course the Lion Hotel.

After dipping in and out of places for an hour she stopped at Ashley's, one of the more recently-established restaurant/coffee shops, ordered a latte and a panini, and took a paperback from her bag. Sitting near a first floor window overlooking the market hall, she started reading. But she found it difficult to concentrate on her book and instead began to think about Connor. In spite of four rehearsals together at Acton Virgil and numerous get-togethers to go through the script for Oklahoma!, he had shown no sign of romantic intentions towards her. She definitely fancied him, but did he fancy her?

And yes, she knew this was the twenty-first century and that the woman did not have to wait around for the man to make the first move. But she had never felt confident enough with Connor to initiate things. She was terrified of making a fool of herself and ruining their friendship. She was waiting, hoping, praying that that first kiss would come, and that he would be the one to lean in towards her with that sparkle in his eyes.

There had been that moment the other night when he had begun a sentence: "Would you . . . " and Vicky had been convinced he was going to say: "Would you mind if I kissed you?" But no. Instead, he asked: "Would you like to hear a joke?" She really had most certainly not wished to hear a joke at that particular moment, but she felt she had no choice but to humour him. And he had continued: "Who can shave twenty-five times a day and still have a beard?" Vicky had looked at him as if he had had some sort of mental breakdown. "I don't know," she said at last. With an expression of triumph, he had declared: "A barber!"

Now, sipping her latte while staring vacantly out of the restaurant window, Vicky allowed her mind to meander back to a time when love was a given. As a child she had been in no doubt about being loved. Her mum and dad would take her on little trips on a Sunday to places like Acton Scott Working Farm Museum or the beautiful hill country of Church Stretton or Stokesay Castle or Much Wenlock or the Severn Valley Railway at Bridgnorth where steam locomotives still reigned supreme. The memory of such day trips warmed her heart now as surely as her latte and panini warmed her stomach. Those trips had all seemed to involve the purchase of tiny souvenirs for her: pencils or notebooks or keyfobs, throwaway items which meant the world to her and which, to this day, still gathered dust among her childhood books and her My Little Pony characters on her shelves. She knew she was loved back then. Finding someone new to love her now was not so easy.

She now considered it extraordinary that, having been on the planet a mere twenty-three years, she could already feel such powerful nostalgia for her own past. Perhaps, she thought, we become nostalgic from the moment our first Christmas annual is handed over by our parents to a charity shop.

As she stepped out of Ashley's she saw Rachael and Joe, arm-in-arm, walking towards her. She had not seen them since her garden party.

"Oh, hi Vic. How are you?" Rachael threw her arms around her friend and squeezed her. As Vicky accepted a kiss on the cheek she felt the brush of a false eyelash whilst being engulfed by a wave of expensive perfume.

"So what you up to?" her friend asked.

"Oh, I've just been having a coffee and something to eat."

"Wish we'd known you were in town. We could have met up for a bite."

"Yeah. We could have."

"Anyway. How's your love life? I hear you're seeing quite a

bit of Zoe's brother. Are you starring in Oklahoma! together or something?"

"Well, we're in this group together and, yes, we're doing a village production of Oklahoma! but I wouldn't say we were *starring* in . . . "

"So what's he like then – Zoe's brother? Are you an item?"

"What's he like? Well, what can I tell you? He's good fun. He's very fond of telling silly jokes," And Vicky suddenly remembered a dream she had had the night following their first trip out to Acton Virgil. It had involved a family of balloons who were all dressed in cowboy gear and in rehearsals for Oklahoma! At the end of the rehearsal, Daddy Balloon had told his son that he had let them all down. "And what else? Let me see. He could do with a good hairdresser," she laughed. "But no. He's very charming, but we're just good friends."

Rachael turned to her boyfriend and said: "Vicky will never settle for anything that's not the best, isn't that right, Vic? When she was a little girl she wanted to marry a prince. I don't think she's ever lowered her expectations since then!"

Vicky grimaced, but Rachael prattled on regardless: "She wants someone tall, dark and handsome, strong and manly. She went out with this guy who worked a JCB digger and he was a bit of all-right, but he still wasn't quite good enough for you, was he, Vic? You really wanted a gladiator, but you ended up with an excavator!"

"Oh very droll, Rachael," said Vicky. "If our amateur dramatics group is putting on a comedy next time, I'll be sure to recommend you."

"Sorry," said Rachael. "Have I gone too far again?"

And Vicky thought to herself: Still very beautiful, still as subtle as a flying hammer.

"I've heard he's very keen on photography," said Joe.

"Well, yeah. I think he is – although I've never seen any of his pictures. I know he has a very impressive camera which he seems to keep in his car all the time."

"Oh really. What sort of a camera. I'm a bit of a photographer myself."

"Oh, I couldn't tell you what it was called. Wait a minute. It's a . . . sounds a bit like a female personal hygiene product."

"A Pentax," said Joe.

"That's the one."

The friends promised each other to link up again soon and then parted company.

In the window of a novelty and joke specialists on her way home, Vicky noticed a kit containing a plastic flower pot and a packet of seeds. In bright red letters, the pack posed a question and provided a solution: "CAN'T GET A BOYFRIEND? – THEN GROW YOUR OWN! – *If you can't get a date, grow the perfect mate!*"

"I may be desperate," she said to herself, "but I'm not *that* desperate."

As she walked on, she comforted herself with the belief that that first kiss from Connor would most surely come sometime soon, that they would eventually marry and have children, and grow old together; that she would take nourishment from his consistently messy hair and consistently silly jokes and his strange love for Rodgers and Hammerstein; that she would be sustained by him just as her mother's chrysanthemum plants found purchase in the rich, dark soil of the garden at South Hermitage.

o o o o o o

"Hospital appears to suit you."

Alastair smiled warmly at his two visitors. "It's very relaxing," he said. "I could get used to this lying around all day and being waited on hand and foot."

"Yeah, well don't get *too* used to it," said Penny, glancing up and down the ward, looking at the other visitors sitting around other beds, one lady pouring orange juice for her recovering husband, another family chatting noisily about the love lives of various professional footballers as exposed in the headlines of tabloid newspapers.

"I'm only kidding," said Alastair. "I'm really looking

forward to coming home and getting back to normal."

Both his wife and his daughter were visiting on this occasion. They had been assured by the doctors that just another day or two and the patient would be allowed home.

"Oh, you'll never guess who came to see me yesterday," said Alastair.

"The prime minister?" said Penny.

"Your fairy-godmother?" said Vicky.

"I'm afraid you're both wrong. It was my old mate Spiky Spencer. Apparently he'd phoned the office on spec to see if we could meet up sometime for a drink, they'd told him I was in hospital, next thing you know he's on a train from Surrey, coming to visit me as a surprise. He brought me this as well." Alastair pointed to a vinyl single propped up next to his 'get well' cards on his bedside cabinet. "It's a rare Donovan single he'd picked up at a record fair. Very thoughtful, don't you think? You know I love Donovan."

Spiky Spencer was an old school pal who – about once a year – would come up to Shrewsbury for a weekend, going out with Alastair for a few pints on the Saturday night and staying the night at the Claytons' place. Spiky (as a little boy he had had Spiky hair and the nickname had stuck) and Alastair shared a love of pop music and films and loved each other's company. They would play little games in the pub to determine who was going to buy the next round. Last time the game had revolved around which movies had featured booksellers. The first one to run out of ideas had to get their wallet out and go to the bar even if they had just bought the last round.

"Okay, booksellers in movies. You have to name the film stars as well as the film. You start, Clayton." Spiky had always called his old friend by his surname.

"Meg Ryan and Tom Hanks in You've Got Mail."

"Good one, Clayton. Okay. Audrey Hepburn in Funny Face."

"Of course. A classic. All right. Anthony Hopkins. 84 Charing Cross Road."

"Mmmm. Nice. Okay. Hugh Grant, Notting Hill."

"Yeah. I'll give you that. Okay. I think that's me done. Looks like I'm getting the drinks." Alastair had risen from his chair and was picking up the empties to return them to the bar when he sat down again and looked at Spiky with an air of victory. "Got it," he said. "Kate Winslet. Eternal Sunshine of the Spotless Mind."

"Oh, bugger," said Spiky. "My round."

The memory of the conversation had made Alastair smile.

"So, anyway. I've invited him over in October. Hope that's okay."

"Of course," said Penny. "He's always been a good friend. He's always welcome." And then Penny started to laugh.

"What's so funny?" asked her husband.

"I've just noticed your fish oil tablets up there on your cabinet. Still taking them, I see. Well, despite your obsessive belief in fish oil and cranberry juice, you still ended up in a hospital bed. It's a bit like the guy who's never smoked, never bothered with alcohol, goes to the gym to work out three times a week, and then he gets hit by a bus. Life's a bitch sometimes."

"Darling, I know I may have made some extravagant claims for the benefits of cranberry juice and Omega 3, but I never said they would stop you from crashing your car."

"However, my sweetheart, your clip-on sunglasses which you normally keep in your glove compartment and which, on this occasion, you'd left at home, might well have helped you to deal with the bright sunshine that day and might have prevented you ending up here."

"Okay, my love. I can't really argue with you there. But you still love me, don't you?"

Penny leant over and gave her husband a kiss.

"Oh, please, you two," said Vicky. "Get a room!"

As Penny and Vicky were leaving the ward, a glamorously attired woman in her late-forties was hovering around a noticeboard in the corridor. Vicky walked straight past her without even glimpsing the stranger, but Penny quickly looked her up and down. This woman looked out of place. She seemed far too beautifully dressed to be hanging around a hospital, and she seemed to be killing time, pretending to read announcements on the noticeboard, trying not to attract attention. The woman looked to Penny like she had spent a great deal of time dying her hair and it looked superb. Age-wise there could not have been that much between them – Penny and this striking-looking female – but this fake reader of noticeboards looked the business, the kind of woman who turned heads, who made men go a little crazy. She was wearing a black silky blouse and was revealing a little too much cleavage. Seeing the woman made Penny feel suddenly old and frumpy. She wondered if she, Penny, ought to make more of an effort on her own appearance.

A minute later and Alastair's wife and daughter were out of the hospital and making their way to the car park.

It was then that the glamorous woman in the corridor made her move. "I'm not too late for visiting time, am I?" she asked a staff nurse.

"There's still five minutes or so," said the nurse, but the woman was already striding towards Alastair's bed as if the answer to her question had been irrelevant.

"Hi," she said.

"Oh, hello, Beth. What are you doing here? Has the office nominated you to come and visit me on behalf of the firm? I've already had visits from Kevin and Terry."

"No-one's nominated me. I just wanted to come and see you."

"Oh, right. Well, that's nice."

"I've brought you a present."

"Oh, lovely."

Beth took from her bag her gift which had been wrapped in sumptuous burgundy and gold paper.

"Oh, really, Beth. You really shouldn't have gone to this much trouble. I don't know what to say."

"You haven't even opened it yet."

A nurse, pushing a wheelchair containing a patient whose

legs were covered in plaster, passed the bottom of Alastair's bed, giving both Alastair and his visitor a friendly smile as she went.

Alastair thought fleetingly how upset his wife would be if the nurse should tell her about the attractive female stranger who had visited her husband. How would he explain that one? Just someone from the office? And why was she dressed so sexily? Because she always dresses sexily?

He unwrapped his gift: a chunky paperback copy of 'The Complete Father Brown: The Enthralling Adventures of Fiction's Best Loved Amateur Sleuth'.

"Blimey! That's great, Beth. That's really great. But how did you know I was a fan of G K Chesterton?"

"I just asked all the guys at work what you were into. Someone suggested you might like an album by some singer-songwriter, and then Kevin told me you liked G K Chesterton. I expect you already have a copy, but . . . "

"Well, I have an old battered copy somewhere at home, but this is . . . this is really something. I'm thrilled."

"Well, in that case, I'm thrilled too."

"I suppose I got into this kind of stuff years ago. I think my first Father Brown book I picked up from a second-hand book shop and I've been hooked ever since."

Beth took his hand, looked straight into his eyes, and said: "Maybe, when you're fully recovered, we could go somewhere together."

There was a long pause as Alastair looked puzzled, trying to think of the correct response. Finally, he said: "Look. Beth. I'm not getting this at all. I'm really not getting this. Firstly, I'm married."

"Yes," she said. "That could be a stumbling block."

Alastair was shocked by her casual phraseology. A stumbling block, for Christ's sake! Was this woman insane? But he composed himself and continued, keeping his voice down so as not to be overheard by passing nurses or the patient in the next bed: "And secondly, you don't even know me. And thirdly, I don't even know you. And fourthly, what in

God's name could a very attractive woman such as yourself see in someone like me anyway? I'm a fifty-four-year-old estate agent and I'm no George Clooney."

"Hey, I think you're lovely, Al. . . and . . ."

There was that "Al" again. Overly familiar. Rather sweet, though. He had to admit he quite liked it. She went on: "And hey, I'm a forty-seven-year-old estate agent. The age gap isn't that big and, if nothing else, we have estate agency in common."

Yep. She was insane. Did she really just say: "We have estate agency in common"?

As he attempted to collect his thoughts, Alastair tried desperately not to keep glancing at Beth's lustrous hair, the sort of hair a man could run his fingers through, and he tried even harder not to keep glancing at her neck and at the way in which her blouse was unbuttoned just slightly too much. He had to steady his nerves. He had to tell her exactly how things were.

"Look, Beth. I'm happily married. I'm really not interested in going out with you. But thank you so much for coming to see me. And thank you so much for the book. I'll treasure it. Okay?"

"Okay."

"Really okay?" he asked, worried that he might have hurt her. But she did not look hurt. Instead, she just let go of his hand and said matter-of-factly: "Okay. I'll go now."

They smiled at each other and she left.

Alastair placed his book of Father Brown detective stories face-down on his bedside cabinet and let out a huge sigh.

And then he thought about that last two minutes.

"Okay. I'll go now," her mouth had said, but her big brown eyes had said: *"So Al. How do you like to spend your evenings?"*

o o o o o o

Alastair awoke the next morning with a dream still lingering at the edge of his consciousness. In the dream he and Beth had run off together and booked into a five-star hotel. There was a spiral staircase. There was a four-poster bed and silk sheets.

As he started to eat his breakfast, the dream was still swirling around his mind. There had been a massive window opening out onto a verandah. The view was lovely. Mountains to the one side, coastline to the other. The air had been the freshest he had ever breathed. His arm and leg were fine again. No discomfort. And Beth had been magnificent.

He pushed his cornflakes around his bowl now as he replayed the dream. He found a tiny burnt fragment of a cornflake and, without thinking, manoeuvred it with his spoon onto the dry upper edge of his dish from which position the fragment bled its burntness, a minuscule slow-motion cascade of dark brown milk. And he stopped eating. And he stared at the brown dribble, and he momentarily thought of his heart then – not the physical organ but the centre of his soul – bleeding in slow-motion, his moral core compromised.

CHAPTER FOUR

PENNY AND ALASTAIR IN OCTOBER

She squeezed a blob of her favourite Crabtree & Evelyn hand lotion into her left palm, breathing in deeply its lavender scent as her hands massaged one another. The kitchen, bathed in afternoon sunlight, was now deliciously warm, partly due to the sun, but mostly due to the homely heat from the oven after the baking of a lemon drizzle cake.

Penny had the house to herself and she was perfectly happy. She amused herself by thinking she could spend a whole week like this, perhaps a month, perhaps a year, just baking cakes, half listening to the radio, drinking tea, dipping into paperbacks from time to time.

Her daughter was out at work, serving fashion-aware customers at Next on the retail park. Her husband too was working, at the ever-so-slightly old-fashioned offices of Penfold, Carroll & Walsh, estate agents, established 1952.

Penny glanced around, drinking in her familiar comforting surroundings: the toaster, the microwave, the roll of patterned kitchen towel, the potted plant, the Fairy Liquid, the kettle, the ceramic key rack by the back door, the 'traditional design' circular clock – white face, black numbers, light brown wooden surround – ticking steadfastly above the window. She loved it all.

Running her fingers across the clean, crumb-free work surface, Penny luxuriated in the smoothness of the laminate. A lover's caress. Without a thought she took a Toblerone chewy chocolate cookie from the packet next to the toaster. Biting into the cookie, she allowed it, so soft, so sweet, to sit on her tongue a while, and then she began to sway and dance as the radio played 'Take Your Mama' by Scissor Sisters, its insistent rhythm filling her with uncomplicated joy.

Well, she loved her daughter, of course she did. And she loved her husband, of course she did (it went without saying). But it was so nice to have the house to herself.

She sprayed kitchen cleaner across the sink unit and draining board, wiping them down while singing along with the radio.

Scissor Sisters had given way to Elton John now. She breathed in the scent of the hand lotion once more, the scent of security, comfort, home. But the lavender was already being chased away by the kitchen cleaner so she applied some more Crabtree and Evelyn.

When alone in the house like this she would often think about Russ Burgess, her first boyfriend, a clever boy who used big words and who was good at technical drawing. He played chess — the only person Penny had *ever* known who played chess.

They had gone out together when they were both seventeen. And for all his serious interests, he had actually been good fun – much more frivolous, she now thought, than Alastair; at least much more frivolous than the Alastair she knew now, the fifty-something Alastair who always seemed to have his mind elsewhere.

She remembered now the long summer afternoons she had spent with Russ, the two of them lying together for hours on a grassy embankment at the furthest faraway edge of the college's recreation grounds. It was peaceful there and they knew they would not be disturbed. They talked for hours. Shared dreams and secrets. Spoke of the future. They kissed and cuddled and sometimes more. They enfolded each other into their two worlds, until the two worlds were one.

Penny had no idea what had since become of Russ, and no particular desire to know. She was not tempted, she told herself now, to track him down through Facebook or Friends Reunited. The past was the past. Nor had she ever mentioned Russ to Alastair. The memories were hers and hers alone. But enough of that, she now told herself, grabbing another Toblerone cookie.

She picked up a DVD of Oklahoma! that her daughter had left lying around and popped it through to the lounge.

Ah, yes. Vicky's lovelife. What on earth was going on with that girl and that pleasant but slightly odd boy from the amateur operatic society? Well, as far as all that business was concerned, there were four clear possibilities, Penny now considered.

One: For whatever reason, Connor simply did not fancy her daughter. Vicky was a lovely girl, but not everyone is attracted to everybody else. If that were the case, what a crazy mixed-up world this would be!

Two: Connor might be very, very, very, very, very, very, very, very, very, very, very, very shy. Maybe he just cannot pluck up the courage to initiate that first kiss and a cuddle.

Three: Connor might be gay. End of story.

Four: Connor may be thinking that he really does not wish to jeopardise a perfect friendship by introducing the notion of a romance between them. A passionate relationship could last two weeks, two months, two years, and yet ultimately fizzle out, and then where would they be? He would have lost the best friend he had ever had. He was not willing to take that risk. Does that sound likely? Well, it was a theory . . .

But all that was for Vicky and Connor to sort out between themselves.

Penny's mind now wandered to thoughts of her husband and the row they had had the other night.

"You do know that if the wind changes, you'll look like that forever."

"Like what?" he had scowled as he came in through the kitchen door, briefcase in hand.

"Oh, God, Alastair. Where's your sense of humour?"

He had had one of those uninspiring days when nothing had gone his way and when he could not think of a single reason why he had gone into the estate agency business in the first place.

"Remember how we used to have a laugh together when we first met?" she had said.

"That was a very long time ago," her husband had replied, not even a hint of a smile upon his lips.

And so the tone for the evening had been set.

She had watched him place his briefcase so carefully in the hall, the case lining up perfectly against the straightness of the wall. Obsessive-compulsive disorder? Alastair had always been like this, but lately it was annoying her and she did not know why. Things like this had never irritated her before, but now she found herself wanting to scream — loudly so that the neighbours would come running and someone would call the police.

He was the kind of man who, having poured himself a bowl of cereals for breakfast, would then take the utmost care to roll down the inner bag to keep in the freshness, and then insert the little flap at the top of the carton, just as recommended by the manufacturer. Did anyone else on the planet do this, wondered Penny. Such characteristics Penny had once found charming, but now they were getting under her skin. Alastair, the man she had once been crazy about, was now just driving her crazy – but not in a good way. "Oh, Alastair," she now said aloud, going for a third cookie but then thinking better of it. "What's become of us? What on earth has become of us?"

He was also a man who was easily pleased (at least superficially), and this too was something Penny used to find endearing about him. Not anymore. His spirits could often be lifted instantly by bright colours or the promise of chocolate.

So just give him a large tube of Smarties and he was in heaven. Part of her had wished she had had a large tube of Smarties stashed away in the pantry, and then she could present them to him and see if his miserable expression would suddenly vanish.

Each of them had always been acutely aware of the big differences between them, differences which, back in their courting days and in the early days of their marriage, they had rejoiced in. But in recent years the differences had started to solidify into battle lines.

He liked The Guardian. She liked the Daily Mail.

He loved coffee, she preferred tea.

He adored his hi-fi and his CD collection. She preferred television.

He was temperamentally suited to the winter. She was a summer person.

He was more of a night owl who then liked a lie-in the next morning, she was never late to bed and always an early riser.

Alastair was a great believer in emailing and (apart from at work) never bothered with paper and envelopes and the Royal Mail anymore. But Penny was fond of sending cards "the old-fashioned way". Pretty little cards. Hand-written messages. She insisted this was much more personal, but, being keen also on renewable resources, she would go out of her way to choose cards printed with soy-based inks on recycled paper.

"So. Are you going to be in a bad mood all night?" she had asked him after tea.

"Sorry, Love. I've had a really crap day. I'm knackered. What can I say?"

"Well, I'm sure you have. And I'm sorry to hear it. But we all have crap days from time to time and we just have to try and put them behind us and have a pleasant evening."

"Thanks for your sympathy."

"Alastair. I know you. I'll bet you weren't in a bad mood on your way home. I'll bet you found some curvaceous lovelies to gawp at from the safety of your car. You're turning into a dirty old man. And please don't tell me it's a mid-life crisis. You're too old to be having a mid-life crisis. I can see you now in my mind's eye: driving home from work, one hand on the wheel, the other stuffing your face with Aero Mint Bubbles, listening to bloody Donovan warbling Catch The Wind, eye-ing up all the talent in town, younger women, prettier women, in their stylish sassy clothes, with their alluring hair and perfect complexions, you letting your imagination run wild, thinking about sex."

He had shaken his head dismissively, but she could still see that he had been startled at the accuracy of the picture she had painted.

"I want a quiet, uncomplicated evening," she had told him. "It's either you and I watching some undemanding telly together or you can bugger off to the pub."

Alastair had chosen the pub.

There might have been a time, not so very long ago, when this would have upset Penny. She might even have shed a tear or two. But not now. She was actually relieved that he had chosen the pub.

That evening, their daughter having gone to the cinema with a few friends, Penny snuggled up on the settee and watched television with only a glass of wine and a large bag of crisps for company. Just for a few seconds, she imagined how her life might have turned out if she had married Russ Burgess instead of Alastair. Would Russ have continued with his interests in chess and technical drawing? Would they still have gone to that grassy embankment for long talks and cuddles?

And down the road at the Belle Vue Tavern, Alastair was sitting in a corner, sipping a pint and reading The Guardian. There was an article entitled: "What makes you happy?" in which half a dozen celebrities had been interviewed about their idea of bliss, and a psychiatrist prattled on about the glass-half-empty versus glass-half-full philosophies. Alastair weighed up the sorts of things which brought him joy. Now, *there* was a question.

A cheap, plastic, poorly manufactured Fort Apache (made in Hong Kong), complete with a dozen tiny US Cavalry soldiers on horseback and a dozen tiny Red Indian warriors on horseback – it must have been among the least expensive toys in the shop – had kept the nine-year-old Alastair happy and occupied for hours during a family summer holiday to Pontins forty-six years earlier. The build-it-yourself fort (and he could still clearly recall the texture of it now) was made up of ribbed, bendy, clip-together strips of brown plastic, made to look like the log-built walls of a wooden Wild West fort but which actually looked more like very cheap chocolate bars. The fort segments and the soldiers and the Indians and the horses had all come in one plastic bag. Some of the tiny horses simply would not stand up no matter how much you twisted their plastic legs.

But, yes, that Fort Apache had made him happy.

To the nine-year-old Alastair, it had been a great fort. They were fine soldiers. They were magnificent Indian warriors. And it had been the first day of a family holiday.

Had he ever been that happy since?

He winced at the question. Oh, come on. Falling in love with Penny. Marrying Penny. The birth of Vicky.

But if he had to make a list of his top ten happiest moments, that day at Pontins would have to be there – nine-year-old Alastair with his plastic Fort Apache, even if some of the horses would not stand up.

o o o o o o

A week after their row, Penny had been dusting upstairs when she noticed the stack of half a dozen books on Alastair's bedside table. At the top of the pile was the book about Donovan which her husband had bought during their last trip to Louth. Just below that was a volume she had not seen before, a brand new paperback, G K Chesterton's 'The Complete Father Brown: The Enthralling Adventures of Fiction's Best Loved Amateur Sleuth'. He must have treated himself, thought Penny, but curiosity got the better of her and she picked up the book to have a closer look.

On the inside-front-cover, she found a hand-written inscription:

To my lovely Al,
Hope you enjoy this as you make a full recovery.
Love and kisses,
Beth
xxx

Penelope rang her mother for advice.
"It's probably nothing at all," said Olivia.
"But why has he kept it a secret from me?"
"Penny, darling, you're imagination is running riot. Let's give him the benefit of the doubt. A man is surely innocent until he is found guilty. Chances are it's not a case of him keeping it a secret. But rather that he hasn't mentioned it because it is insignificant. It's some woman in the office who has sent him a gift because they're work colleagues and good mates, but nothing more."
"But Mum. I mean – *love and kisses*? Come on!"
"People always write stuff like that on get well cards and suchlike. It doesn't mean a thing."
"But Mum. I mean . . . *To my lovely Al*? . . . And, to be honest with you, we haven't been getting on too well, lately. Since he came out of hospital, he's been different somehow. Not so much fun as he used to be. I don't know if it was the accident or what, but . . ."
"Penny. Believe me, darling. If you're not careful all this could blow up in your face and you'll end up regretting the day you picked up that book. Just leave it alone, for heaven's sake. Don't keep digging. You'll just hurt yourself and ruin everything."
"What do you mean?"
"I mean this is probably nothing at all. Alastair isn't the kind to have an affair. That's the first thing. The second thing is: you dig and you dig and you dig and you end up confronting him about it and – just supposing there is something in it, just

perhaps the fact that they've been for a couple of drinks together or they just like the same kind of movies – before you know it, he's getting all defensive and you're on the attack and it all ends up in one great enormous bust-up. He says things he doesn't mean. You say things back to him that you don't really mean. It all gets ugly. You hurt one another. Then, suddenly, there's no going back. You've poisoned what you had. Think of that, darling. Think of your precious marriage. And think of dear sweet Vicky. For God's sake, Penny, don't go buggering it all up over a silly inscription in a book."

"Oh, I don't know, Mum. Perhaps I should have married Russ Burgess."

"Don't be such a bloody fool, Penny. You love Alastair and Alastair loves you. End of story. *I* can see that. Why can't *you* see it?"

A few nights later and it was history repeating itself. Penny – who had taken her mother's advice and had said nothing to her husband about the inscription in the book – went for the quiet night in in front of the telly. Alastair took himself down to the Belle Vue Tavern. This time, sitting across the way from Alastair in a cosy corner of the pub were three of his acquaintances: Frank the window cleaner, John the retired baker and Paul the postman. John and Paul were deep in conversation while Frank was absorbed in a newspaper crossword. "We'd invite you to join us but you look comfy enough over there with The Guardian," said Frank.

"Oh, no, that's okay. Thanks anyway. I wouldn't want to interrupt you. I'm just catching up on a bit of reading myself."

"Thought so."

"Might join you later, though."

"Sure."

Alastair just wanted some time to himself. His mood of late had not been improved by news that his best friend Spiky Spencer had had to cancel his promised October visit to Shrewsbury. The visit would now have to be re-arranged in the new year. But this was not the main reason for Alastair's gloom. He knew that he and Penny were drifting apart, but he just could not figure out why. Nor could he see any easy solution. Flowers and chocolates were never going to do it. Not this time. It was going to take more than that. But he was stuck. He was lost. He did not know how to get back.

He sipped at his bitter, glancing across at Frank and John and Paul. He envied them a little bit. Friendship. It was something he was not very good at. There had only ever been Spiky Spencer, his dear old friend from childhood days. And he lived in Surrey now and they saw each other only a couple of times a year.

"At the shops without your scrap of paper."

Alastair looked up from his Guardian. "I'm sorry, Frank. What was that?"

"Nine across. At the shops without your scrap of paper."

"Oh, I see. How many words?"

"One."

Alastair played with his beermat for a moment. "Listless," he said.

"Brilliant," said Frank. "Thanks for that."

All Alastair had wanted had been a couple of hours alone with his thoughts. The Guardian was only ever intended as a prop so that he did not appear to be a complete down-and-outer, sitting in the pub with not a soul to talk to. But now he found himself helping Frank with his crossword.

He thought fleetingly about moving down the road to The Masonic or the Prince of Wales. And then he had a sudden flashback to the very first time he had clapped eyes on the Prince of Wales.

He had been twelve and was heavily into model railways at the time. His own layout had been modest, just an oval of track with a couple of sidings, a station, a signal box, a tiny village comprising three thatched cottages and a pub. A diesel locomotive. Half a dozen freight trucks. His dad had taken him to the home of a work colleague who had in his loft a massive layout boasting a dozen trains, plus bridges, tunnels, two stations, a small town, a level crossing, roads with cars and buses on them, woodland, a river – it was amazing. After an hour or so of being dazzled by this fine example of a model railway, Alastair and his father had left the house and walked to the nearest pub, the Prince of Wales. Alastair, being only a child, had to sit outside with a bottle of Vimto while his dad went inside for a couple of pints. A happy memory, the adult Alastair now thought.

But why were all these childhood memories coming to him now? Was this how it worked? When life as a grown-up was going down the toilet, you comforted yourself with thoughts of years gone by?

"A self-governed region that ebbs and flows. Three words. What dya think, Alastair?"

"A self-governed region that ebbs and flows? – State of flux."

"Bloody hell. You're good at this."

"Got to be good at something," said Alastair, reckoning he was not too good at being a husband right now. He pictured his wife back home, watching the telly, perhaps shedding a tear over the state of their marriage. She was a fine wife, loving and generous and faithful, and she was also a fantastic mother to their daughter, and a damn good teacher as well. Alastair knew full well that Penny considered herself to be merely a "good" teacher, but not a great one; too smart to worry overmuch about the mediocre Ofsted report, too recalcitrant to ask "how high?" when the head teacher asked her to jump.

The primary school across town which was Penny's place of work was a friendly enough place with a committed staff, but many of the children were from disadvantaged homes, and having to inspire them every day could be quite a challenge. Asked by her friends if she still enjoyed her job, Penny would always say: "Oh, it's just fine . . . but if I ever win the lottery, I'll pack it all in in a heartbeat." Alastair smiled to himself at the thought. What the hell was he doing here in the pub when he should be at home supporting her?

"Here's one for you, Alastair." It was Frank again.

"Go on."

"Selection of different kinds of things – now completely exhausted. Three words."

Alastair took a sip of his beer, looked up, and said: "Out of sorts."

CHAPTER FIVE

BACKHOE BILLY, BACK-AGAIN BETH

"Connor. Would you do us a favour and see who that is at the front door?"

Connor was not used to taking instructions from Vicky's dad, but Vicky was helping her mum prepare a meal in the kitchen and Alastair Clayton was sitting in his favourite armchair, surrounded by paperwork which he had brought home from the office – piles of leaflets and documents about houses for sale.

"Sure," said the young man from the Acton Virgil Amateur Operatic Society, feigning enthusiasm. With some reluctance, and feeling he was being 'used' in a way he did not much care for, Connor put down the newspaper he had been looking at and went to the front door.

A man in his early twenties – about the same age as Connor in fact – stood at the door. "Hi," he said. "It's a nice evening isn't it?"

"Er . . . yes. I suppose it is," said Connor, idly looking up and down South Hermitage and wondering if this person might be a Jehovah's Witness. "It's chilly, but then it is

October so . . ."

The stranger continued: "Is Vicky in?"

"She might be."

"Oh good. I've come to see her."

"I'm sorry. Who are you?"

"I'm her boyfriend."

"I don't think so."

"Yes. I am. I'm her boyfriend."

Connor leant against the doorframe with an outstretched arm, as if blocking the way, and said firmly: "No. You're not."

"What do you mean?"

"What do *you* mean – 'what do I mean'? I mean you're *not* her boyfriend."

"I mean: why is it so hard for you to believe that I'm her boyfriend?"

"Because *I'm* her boyfriend," said Connor, sounding slightly more aggressive than he had intended.

"Oh," said the stranger.

"Is that it then – just 'oh'?"

"Well, all right then. Let me start again. I'm her ex-boyfriend."

"Well, why didn't you say that in the first place?"

The stranger looked Connor straight in the eye for a moment and then said: "Because when you're introducing yourself to someone for the first time, 'boyfriend' sounds a heck of a lot better than 'ex-boyfriend'."

"I've got news for you, mate. Ex-boyfriend sounds a heck of a lot better than 'boyfriend' to me."

"Well, yeah . . . I can see . . ."

"Wait a minute. Wait a minute," said Connor. "I know who you are now. You're the JCB digger operator from the other side of town. That's how Vicky described you."

"Yeah. Okay. Let's start again," said the visitor. "I'm Billy." He offered his hand to shake Connor's, but Connor did not move an inch. Instead, he said: "Has it occurred to you that Vicky might not want to see you?"

"I think she should be the judge of that, don't you?"

The two young men stared at one another for a few moments and then Billy said: "Well? Are you going to invite me in?"

And with that, but with no smile upon his face, Connor lowered his arm and allowed Billy to step inside.

"Good God!" declared Alastair, looking up from his armchair. "If it isn't Backhoe Billy."

"Hello Alastair. How are you?"

Connor interrupted: "Sorry . . . Back-what?"

"Backhoe Billy," said Billy. "That's my nickname. Because I drive a backhoe loader. Y'know? The big digger?"

Connor looked confused.

Alastair continued as if Connor were invisible. "Come in. Come in, Billy. Take a seat, please. It's great to see you. Vicky *will* be pleased. Go on, mate. Take a seat. Would you like a cup of tea or a beer or something?"

Billy sat down on the sofa, in the exact spot Connor had been sitting a few moments before.

"That's awfully kind of you, Alastair. Yeah. Okay. I'll have a beer."

Connor stood with his back to the lounge door, helplessly watching the scene unfold before him.

Alastair called the women of the family and Penny and Vicky appeared, both clearly pleased to see Billy. Then Alastair fetched a can of lager, opened it, poured the lager into a glass and presented it to their guest.

"I've got something for you guys," announced Billy. And he produced from a small carrier bag a packet of Smarties for Alastair and two small boxes of chocolates, one for Vicky, the other for her mum. He turned to Connor and said with relish: "I'm sorry, mate. I don't have anything for you."

Stung into action, Connor decided to fight back. "This young chap here introduced himself just now as your boyfriend, Vick. So I had to put him right and tell him that *I'm* your boyfriend now."

"Well, how dare you?"

"I was about to tell him the same thing," said Connor.

"I wasn't talking to Billy," said Vicky, clearly annoyed and staring at Connor. "I was talking to you."

"But . . ."

"How dare you, Connor? How dare you describe yourself as my boyfriend? You've never even kissed me. You've never shown any romantic feelings towards me. After weeks and weeks of going out to Acton Virgil together, learning lines together, singing together, feeding the bloody cat together. You've never expressed any interest. And now you have the bloody audacity to describe yourself as my boyfriend? I just don't understand you. I really don't understand you at all."

Connor looked down at his shoes.

Penny and Alastair shot glances at one another.

"Billy, it's really nice to see you," continued Vicky. "Really nice. But it's been a long time. And you're not my boyfriend either. Your licence has expired. You can't just walk back in here and expect everything to be just the same as it was. We had a big row. Remember? We split up. Do you remember any of this? Neither of you are my boyfriend. I don't have a boyfriend. Now, if you'll all excuse me, I'm going to my room."

o o o o o o

Down at the Belle Vue Tavern that evening, Alastair, doodled aimlessly in the margins of his Guardian as he munched on his salt and vinegar crisps and sipped his pint. Miserable weeks were building into a series of miserable months and he was beginning to hate his work. He hated the monotony of it all. He hated the fact that he had been doing the same thing for years. He hated the staleness of his office. He hated the uninspiring view from the window, the bland pictures on the wall, the bloody awful calendar depicting birds of the British Isles. Alastair would concede that they were expertly-taken photographs, but they did nothing for him personally. July: a coot on the river. August: the common chaffinch sitting on a branch. September: barn owls. October:

great tits feeding at a bird table. He knew it was a failing in him, but he could never get excited about natural history. David Attenborough's programmes would always send him to sleep.

"Blimey, Alastair. You seem to be down here more than we are these days – and that's saying something." It was John the retired baker at the head of his little gang, Frank the window cleaner and Paul the postman.

"Oh, hi there fellas."

"Fancy joining us for a game of dominoes?"

Alastair glanced down at his dog-eared Guardian, looked up at John and said: "Oh, dya know what? I just might do that."

o o o o o o

Vicky was on a break at Next. She picked up a fashion magazine that had been lying on a chair in a backroom of the store where she often enjoyed a half-hour away from the shopfloor. She drank coffee and ate a Toffee Crisp as she flicked through the pages. On one page was a photograph of three men, each one dressed in a casual shirt and lightweight trousers, looking as if they were about to take an early evening stroll along the seaside promenade. Hairline rules pointed to the shirts, the trousers, the footwear. At the source of each hairline was a bulletpoint offering descriptions of the garment, details of the shops from which you could buy them, and the prices.

The first man pictured, skinny, hair dishevelled, looked not unlike Connor. Vicky found a pen and wrote 'Connor' above the picture.

The second man was not her type at all and she drew a big cross through him.

The third man, if you scrunched up your eyes, could, at a push, be Billy, she decided. She smiled and wrote 'Billy' above his head. Then she drew her own hairline rules and her own bulletpoints.

Below 'Connor' she wrote:

- Loves Shrewsbury
- Loves Rodgers and Hammerstein
- Tells awful jokes
- Bit pretentious
- Difficult to work out

Below Billy she wrote:

- Loves football
- Loves heavy rock
- Tells it like it is
- Heart in the right place
- Easy to work out

And then she wrote at the foot of the page:
'Billy just ahead on points!'

o o o o o o

December had arrived with all the drama of a leaf falling from a tree. It was another dreary Monday morning in the offices of Penfold, Carroll and Walsh, and Alastair glanced about him, at the pile of papers on his desk, at the chipped Batman mug in which he kept all his pens and pencils, at the Birds of the British Isles calendar on the wall.

He reflected upon the usual boring breakfast he had had an hour before: his two "very good for you" Weetabix, his "anti-cardiovascular diseases" cranberry juice, and his "cholestorol-busting" Omega 3 tablet.

Suddenly, there was an overly-enthusiastic voice in his head.

"I'm showing a couple round a house in Harlescott at 11.30, but I'm free for a couple of hours after that. So what do you fancy doing, Al? We could have lunch together."

Alastair looked up to see an ample bosom in a tight white T-shirt. Embarrassed, he glanced away to the Birds of the

British Isles calendar and saw two great tits.

He sighed. "I beg your pardon, Beth. What was that you were saying? I haven't really woken up yet."

She put the offer of lunch to him a second time. He mumbled something about being rather too busy to meet up, but perhaps some other time. She said she would be in Poppy's having a baked potato if he should change his mind.

At one o'clock, Alastair was in Claremont News, his favourite town centre newsagents which was housed in a quaint little Victorian building sandwiched tightly between two sixties structures. He had been coming to this newsagents since he was a little boy. This is where he had once bought his American comics: Spider Man, Superman, Batman. He now picked up a copy of Shindig!, a magazine aimed at ageing pop fans and rooted mainly in the pre-punk era. This suited him well.

Alastair loved pop and rock but had never been into punk. It was a genre that had, for the most part, passed him by – or, like a punk fan's spit spat high, had flown over his head without making an impact upon his otherwise catholic tastes. The yobbish shouting associated with the movement, the profanities, the sneering, snarling and grunting, the saliva projecting, and the predominantly tuneless thrashing of the movement's vanguard – the Sex Pistols, The Clash – he had found decidedly unappealing. On the other hand, he had a deep and profound love for the music of the sixties and early seventies. He bought the magazine along with a Mars bar and a bag of crisps – his intended lunch.

But after leaving the newsagents, he drifted, without thinking, towards The Square and eventually to Poppy's, the restaurant Beth had mentioned earlier. She would be in there about now, he thought, eating her baked potato. What possible harm could it do, to pop in and join her?

Beth beamed when she saw Alastair. "So you made it then?"

"Well, I was just ... "

"Great to see you. It's not a lot of fun, having lunch on

your own."

"Oh, I don't know," said Alastair, imagining himself happily scoffing his Mars bar and crisps back at his desk. But no. Perhaps the chocolate bar and the salt and vinegar could keep for another day. He smiled and said: "I actually don't mind my own company sometimes, you know? It gives you a chance to think."

A waitress appeared.

"I'll have a baked potato like my friend here, please. With coleslaw. Er . . . and a coffee."

"Filter coffee or just ordinary?"

"Just ordinary."

"A mug or a cup?"

"A mug."

"Milky or . . . "

"Milky please."

When the waitress was out of earshot, he said: "Blimey. It's like Twenty Questions." And Beth laughed.

Alastair took in the dark-oak-panelled walls, the beams in the ceiling, and the rickety staircase. He plucked a sachet of demerara sugar from the small bowl before him and began messing with it nervously.

"Did you know that Captain John Benbow is buried just over the road in the churchyard of old St Chad's?"

"No. I didn't know that," said Beth, snatching the sachet of sugar from him and placing it back in the bowl. "Nothing to do with Admiral Benbow?"

"Completely different chaps – although some think John may have been the admiral's uncle. Difficult to say for sure, I think. Anyway. Admiral Benbow was a sailor – obviously. He fought against the French in the 1690s. Decades before that though, Captain John Benbow was a Parliamentarian soldier in the civil war. In 1645 he became celebrated for his part in the capture of Shrewsbury from the Royalists. But then, years later, for some reason he changed sides and, after the Battle of Worcester, was captured by Cromwell's men. He was found guilty of treason and was eventually shot by firing squad –

ironically at Shrewsbury Castle."

"Gosh, Al. You know a lot about history, don't you?"

"Yeah. Well, my wife and I, we both . . . " And he suddenly felt awkward and embarrassed, talking about his wife.

"Look, Beth. I'll be your friend. Okay. But it can never be anything more than that." And even as he said this, Alastair knew something had changed. For weeks now he had been able to more or less ignore Beth in the office. He had trained himself not to think about her too much. Even though his relationship with his wife was going through what people often referred to as 'a sticky patch', Alastair knew that running into the arms of another would surely spell disaster. He knew all this. And yet here he was sitting in a restaurant with Beth, feeling that a line had already been crossed.

"I'll tell you what," said Beth. "Let's do this again sometime. And we'll just see how it goes."

o o o o o o

In common with most other British towns and cities, Shrewsbury had expanded significantly in the years that followed World War II, its shape and character changing in the process. (This simple fact would often be dutifully ignored – along, come to that, with the comings and goings of the last five hundred years – whenever the tourism office of the present day insisted on describing Shrewsbury as "a medieval town".)

Even in the few short years between 1945 and 1952, 422 new houses were built on the Crowmoor estate, another 67 in Albert Road, 138 in Oakfield Road, 238 at Springfield, and 136 at Meadow Farm, Harlescott. Thousands more were on their way.

But it was in one of these early newcomers, a 1950s semi, that Back-hoe Billy lived with his two best friends. The three of them rented the place between them. It suited their needs well enough. They had allowed the back garden to become overgrown and they were not the tidiest of young men, but no-one ever seemed to complain about this – not their neighbours, whose own gardens were almost as bad, and not the friends they would occasionally invite round for evenings of beer, a Chinese takeaway, and football on the telly.

The house stood in a bland street on the Harlescott estate in the north of the town; a more industrial, less pretty, more working class part of Shrewsbury, and two substantial bus rides away from the refined and handsome Belle Vue – Billy did not own a car.

He stood one morning before the bathroom mirror, having a shave, mulling over for the umpteenth time his reception at the Clayton home six weeks earlier. It had, he conceded, not been a *complete* success. Fair enough. But nor had it been an utter disaster either. Her mum and dad had been friendly enough, but Vicky had been angry and defensive. Connor, on the other hand, had been understandably hostile towards him. Billy had taken away from South Hermitage that night a series of confusing signals which would require contemplation. His conclusions now were something like this: Alastair and Penny still liked him. New-kid-on-the-block Connor most certainly did not like him. But, interestingly, Connor was not the 'new boyfriend' he had believed himself to be. Which gave Billy considerable hope. Vicky, meanwhile, might be confused and annoyed, but she had not closed the door completely on a reconciliation with Billy.

The JCB driver from the other side of town swilled his face and began to plan Phase Two of his "Get Back With Vicky" campaign.

o o o o o o

Alastair was playing with a sachet of sugar again. This was his third lunchtime meeting with Beth at Poppy's and it was becoming a habit.

"I'm toying with the idea of getting a cat. What do you think?" she asked.

"Well, they can be good company." Alastair knew she lived alone. That she was divorced. That she was a little lonely. "We have one. Chesterton."

"Oh. After your favourite author."

"That's right."

"Can you stop messing with that sachet?"

Alastair placed it back in the bowl.

"So you would recommend a cat, then?"

"Oh, I don't know, Beth." He still found he had to make a conscious effort to concentrate on her face and not her bosom while talking with her. She continued to wear blouses which were just a little too revealing.

"You don't know if a cat would be right for me?"

Alastair knew that what Beth really needed was a man, not a cat. But he could hardly suggest such a thing.

Beth gave up on an answer and decided to enjoy her omelette instead.

Alastair also began eating in earnest while glancing around at the oak-panelled walls and the historic beams.

"Read any good books lately?" he asked after minutes had passed by without a word between them.

"Now there's a classic chat-up line," she said.

"Sorry."

"As a matter of fact, I've started reading up on local history. I'm finding out about the Roundheads being allowed through the gates by a traitor. The soldiers coming up St Mary's Waterlane. And that's why the restaurant there is called Traitor's Gate."

"I must take you and show you Captain Benbow's gravestone in Old St Chad's graveyard sometime."

"Yeah. But I don't think we have time today. We ought to be getting back."

As they stepped outside the restaurant, Beth pulled Alastair towards her and kissed him on the lips.

They walked back to the office together in silence.

CHAPTER SIX

HAPPIEST OF MOMENTS

Christmas had come and gone in the Clayton household with comparatively little magic involved in the festivities at South Hermitage – which was, thought Vicky now as she applied her make-up, not how it was supposed to be. Every Christmas she could recall had been special in some way, from those of her happy childhood when she and her mum would always leave a glass of sherry for Santa and a carrot for his reindeer before going to bed on Christmas Eve, right up to recent times, like last year when the three of them had laughed and cried together as a family over a selection of their favourite festive films.

It had always been a warm and loving time of year, but there had been something lacking this time. And Vicky could not figure out why. Had there been a short supply of good humour between the three of them? Had she detected a certain chill between her normally very affectionate parents? She dabbed a little perfume on her neck and behind her ears and turned her thoughts to other matters.

Connor would be calling for her soon and driving her out

to Acton Virgil for another rehearsal with The Pigeons. She did not know for how much longer she could keep this up – this studied indifference towards a young man for whom she had feelings (and she would admit those feelings only to herself). And whether or not those feelings were stronger than the ones she still felt for Billy she could not determine. But there was something there nonetheless and it was exhausting having to pretend otherwise.

Alastair was in his favourite armchair, pretending to read The Guardian. But actually he also was thinking about what a drab Christmas they had just experienced. He considered that if there had been some kind of device to measure the love in the Clayton household during December, it would have revealed levels to have been abnormally low.

He knew that the arrival of Beth in his life, as a friend and perhaps as something more than a friend, was a factor in all of this. But he was equally convinced that Penny was nowhere near as loving as she had been. And he knew that these two issues could so easily result in disaster.

He picked up the framed photograph of himself and Penny, the one taken at the fun fair in Skegness all those years ago, and he saw how very young they both looked in that happy summer's day image. Candy floss, music, the smell of hamburgers, the laughter of children.

Did he have it in him to bury all those memories and threaten the homelife he now had by embarking on some silly adventure with Beth?

There had been only that one kiss – outside Poppy's when Beth had seized the moment. And that minute of crazy impetuousness on her part had never since been mentioned by either of them. Sometimes, it was easy to pretend it had never happened. Other times, Alastair enjoyed playing the moment over and over in his mind.

Yes, he thought, there was undoubtedly a certain vanity present in Beth's complex personality – the sexy hairstyle, lipstick, the exposed cleavage – but there was something else too. And he had seen it in those awkward exchanges across the sachets of sugar in Poppy's. Beyond the apparent self-confidence of this desirable woman there was a vulnerability, a timidity even, which he found deliciously attractive.

Just then, Alastair's daughter breezed into the lounge with a cheerful "Hi, Dad!" and watched as her father carefully put back the photograph.

"Hello, Sweetheart. Off to rehearsals again?"

"Yeah. Not long now before the actual shows begin. Only a few weeks."

"We'll be there."

"I might be able to wangle some free tickets for you and Mum."

"Oh, I think your mother and I can just about stretch to the cost of a couple of tickets."

"Fair enough."

"And don't forget your grandma is coming over especially for the show. So it had better be good."

"It'll be even better than the film, Dad. You wait and see!"

"Mmmmm. You smell nice."

"Oh, it's a Next one. I get discount. Nice, though, isn't it?"

"Lovely. Still trying to impress Connor?"

"Oh, I don't know, Dad. I think I may have given up in that direction. He's had his chances."

"Well, if I were you, if he shows no interest in you, I'd give Billy a call and ask him out to the pictures."

"It's not that easy."

"It never is."

There was a lull in the conversation and Alastair turned the pages of his newspaper with a feigned sense of purpose.

Finally, Vicky asked: "Is everything all right with you and Mum."

"God, Love. Whatever made you ask *that*?"

"It's just that Christmas felt a little bit strange. Like we were all just going through the motions."

"Funny. I was just thinking the same thing."

"So things *are* okay between you."

"Oh, yeah. We've been married a long time now, Vick. Your mum and I can't be lovey-dovey *all* the time."

"It's just that, you know . . . as a family . . . we don't seem to have so much fun as we used to do. Do you remember a couple of Christmases ago when you and I ended up at The Exchange with a whole bunch of girlfriends of mine?"

"Yeah, it's a wonder I didn't get arrested. A middle-aged man surrounded by all those raunchy young ladies . . . Bloody good night, though."

Alastair recalled the evening with relish, smiling at his daughter. "Just a few nights before Christmas, wasn't it? You invited me along and – much to your astonishment – I accepted."

"That's right. Mum didn't fancy it. Of course she wouldn't. Not exactly her cup of tea. So she just wanted a quiet night in with the telly, but you were really up for it. Remember we climbed up a fire escape and ended up on stage with the band. And the lead singer ended up naked apart from a Santa Claus hat and a Christmas sock over his willy?"

They both laughed.

"Remind me, Vick. Why did we have to climb a fire escape?"

She stood in front of the lounge mirror, brushing her hair. "Well, I knew one of the bouncers on the door so he let us in for free – me, you, Rachael, Zoe – that's Connor's sister, yeah? Plus Jenny and Lizzie Tyler. We all got in for nowt. But then we couldn't go through the main door of course because we didn't actually have any tickets, so my bouncer friend said 'go that way – go through the ladies' toilets, out the back door and up the fire escape', And so we did. Ladies' toilet. Back door. Fire escape. And then into the upper room where the band was playing."

"God, yes. I'd forgotten. I actually had to walk through the ladies' toilets. I really *could* have been arrested."

"Yeah. And then we found ourselves at the back of the stage while the band was still belting out Clash classics, definitely definitely definitely not Mum's cup of tea. All at deafening volume. And we went down these little steps from the stage and into the hall. Quite a night."

Vicky sat down to put her shoes on.

Alastair found he could not stop smiling, just savouring the memory, but still silently asking himself: How could an evening so packed with life, so stacked high with beer and hope and salt and vinegar crisps, so crammed to the rafters with Christmas spirit and loud rock music and fire escapes and a naked singer and companionship and connection and Scampi Fries and love . . . how could such an evening still be replete with loss? And the answer could only be that even in the happiest of moments there is sadness; even when we have everything, we know it cannot last.

o o o o o o

On the drive out to Acton Virgil, Vicky noticed that Connor had two new car stickers attached to the top corner of the windscreen, one facing outwards, one facing inwards. They were identical and – in red letters on a white background – declared: *'THE PIGEONS – Amateur operatics flying high!'* – and there was a little cartoon pigeon flapping merrily above a little cartoon town. Vicky wondered if pigeons ever actually flew high. She had only ever seen them fluttering from flower bed to flower bed on the pedestrianised Pride Hill in the town centre, hoping for breadcrumbs or the remnants of a sandwich from Greggs. She found the idea of such creatures soaring eagle-like above a town quite comical.

The operatic society had been formed from humble beginnings in 1952 as nothing more than a modest comedy drama group, originally staging only farces and pantomimes, and embracing to begin with a handful of enthusiasts from no further afield than the host village. But as its membership grew in numbers, in experience, and in confidence, the society looked outwards and brought into the fold some fine musicians, dedicated front-of-house people, lighting, sound and wardrobe specialists from a much wider geographical area, drawing talent from not only half a dozen surrounding villages, but also from the towns of Whitchurch, Wem and Shrewsbury.

Over the years there had been various attempts to move the Pigeons' headquarters to one of the larger centres, but such proposals had always eventually lost out to the argument that the heart and soul of this society would forever be associated with the picture-postcard village of Acton Virgil.

Oklahoma! was to be staged at Acton Virgil Village Hall in early March. Posters were up all across north Shropshire and tickets were already selling well.

The Killers were playing on Connor's CD player as he turned west off the B5476 onto a quiet road flanked by tall hedges.

"Do you remember, we were playing this CD on our first trip out here?" said Connor.

"Of course I remember," said Vicky. "You know that was four and a half months ago, don't you?"

"There's no need to sound so aggressive, Vick. I'm trying to be nice."

"Oh, you're trying to be nice."

"Yes. Yes, I am."

"Connor, I just don't get you."

He pulled into a layby and switched off the ignition. "I was trying to be romantic," he said.

"But why? Why now? What's changed?"

Instead of answering, he leant across and kissed her.

After a moment, he said: "I know I've been a bit of a pillock. I realise that. But, you know?"

"What, Connor? For God's sake, just spit it out, will you?"

"Look, Vick. I've really liked you from the moment I first saw you. But it's complicated."

"Complicated? How? How is it complicated?"

"My emotions have been all over the place these last few months. I suppose I wasn't sure whether I wanted to start something, you know, serious."

"Well, at least you're talking about it now. That's a starting point. Maybe we can build on this."

He leant over and kissed her again, this time more passionately. She pushed him away.

"Okay, Tiger. One step at a time, all right?" she said. "Having messed me about all this time, you can't just suddenly start being something else. Let's just cool it a little bit. Let's talk some more over the coming days. Let's try being honest with one another. How about that? Let's begin by giving up any secrets we might have. And then we'll see where we end up."

"Sure," he said quietly. And, after a moment of indecision, he switched on the ignition and drove on towards Acton Virgil.

As they travelled, Vicky remembered the glossy magazine article featuring pictures of men in casual shirts and lightweight trousers. She recalled the lists she had made of things she liked about (a) Connor and (b) Billy, and she remembered that, having weighed it all up, she had put Billy ahead on points. But then, she wondered: when it comes to affairs of the heart, how could a stupid points system ever help anyone?

She glanced across at the handsome but annoyingly enigmatic Connor as Acton Virgil Village Hall came into view.

o o o o o o

It was the third week of January and Penny had gone over to Louth to spend some 'quality time' with her mother.

"Christmas just wasn't the same without . . . I was going to say: Christmas just wasn't the same without you and Dad being with us." Penny placed her mug of tea onto the 'Lincolnshire scenes' coaster next to the golden wedding anniversary photograph of her parents. "And I know we're never going to have another Christmas with Dad, but it would have been really lovely to have had you with us, Mum. Truth be told, it was a pretty miserable Christmas for us this time."

Olivia gave her daughter a warm, understanding smile. "Look, Pen. I wasn't really up to the journey this time, and you can imagine – first Christmas without your Dad around – it was not easy for me at all. Not at all. I didn't really feel like celebrating. I just wanted a quiet one. So when your Auntie

Barbara and Uncle Colin invited me, it sounded just the job. And, as it turned out, it *was* just the job. Nice and quiet. A good few glasses of sherry and lots of rubbishy television. Good company. That did the trick."

"But next Christmas you must come to us," said Penny.

"I have something even better in mind."

"How do you mean?"

"I'm thinking of coming to live in Shrewsbury."

"Oh, that would be fantastic, Mum."

"Do you think your Alastair would be able to stand it?"

"You know full well he thinks the world of you."

"And I'll be able to see a heck of a lot more of you and that beautiful grand-daughter of mine."

"Well, of course, you'll be coming over to see her in Oklahoma! in a few weeks' time. That'll be lovely. A bright golden haze on the meadow and all that. But tell me more about your plans to move to Shrewsbury. This is all very exciting. What's brought this on?"

Olivia told her daughter that she believed she would be lonely staying in Louth, that although Barbara and Colin were wonderful and that although she had two or three good friends living locally, she was concerned about the years ahead. "I don't want to feel lonely," she said. "It's not a nice feeling." She sipped her tea and went on: "And I think if I had you and Alastair and our precious Vicky just down the road – y'know, maybe just a short bus ride away, I wouldn't want to be living on top of you all the time – then I wouldn't feel lonely any more. I could pop round and do some ironing for you. You could just pop round for tea and biscuits instead of having to endure that long journey across country. We could go shopping together. I could go shopping with Vicky if she didn't find it too embarrassing to be out with an old lady."

"This is really great news, Mum. This is just brilliant. You've made my day."

"And besides, the garden is far too big for me. I can't cope with it. You know it was always your father's domain. Come to that, this house is too big for me as well. I need to downsize.

And if I'm going to downsize, I might as well do it in Shrewsbury and be close to my family."

Later that day, as they were both half-watching the teatime news, Olivia asked her daughter the question she had been trying to pluck up the courage to ask since she had first arrived.

"So anyway, Love. How are you and Alastair getting along these days?"

"And if I said we weren't getting along at all, would you change your mind about moving to Shrewsbury?"

"Don't be silly, Pen."

"Sorry. Well, no, it's not great between us, Mum. It's not all rockets, bells and poetry."

"Beg your pardon."

"It's a Mamas and Papas song."

"Oh."

"And because we're not exactly hitting it off at the moment, it's affecting all three of us, I think. As a family, you know? We're finding it harder to laugh together. We don't have the same fun that we used to have."

"So the honeymoon period is over, then?"

"I think the honeymoon period has been over for nearly thirty years, Mum."

"But I know you love Alastair and I know he loves you, Pen."

"I think you're right. We're just going through a rough patch. And, before you ask me again, I haven't confronted him about the inscription in that book. For now, I'm pretending not to have seen it. He *does* go down to the Belle Vue Tavern a lot, but I'm pretty sure he's not having an affair. He just goes down there to read the Guardian or to see his mates."

"Oh, well thank goodness for that."

"He might be thinking about having an affair, but right now I see no evidence of him actually having one."

"Perhaps *I* should talk to him, Pen?"

"Blimey, Mum."

"I'll bet I could make him see sense."

"Mmmm. I'll let you know on that one."

"Oh, I'm so sorry things are difficult for you at the moment. And I'm so sorry you had a disappointing Christmas. You lot are famous for your great Christmases."

"Oh, I know. Alastair has this thing about 'magic'. Even though none of us are religious at all – at least not as far as organised religion is concerned, Alastair does like to create or inject some magic into our Christmases. When he is in one of his pompous moods, he will describe himself as a romantic agnostic, whatever the hell that is supposed to mean. He'll tell you that he sort of believes, some of the time, in a wishy-washy god of some kind. That he believes a little bit in some sort of life after death. And that he thinks miracles *can* happen. But it's all awfully vague and non-conformist. His own personal vision has absolutely no time for a virgin birth or for a three-in-one God: the father, the son and the holy ghost. But he does like his magic. He likes a bit of mysticism and a bit of non-specific spirituality. And I'm afraid that was sorely missing from our Christmas this time."

"Well, I'll tell you what, Pen. When I move across to Shrewsbury, I'll bring a bit of non-specific spirituality with me."

o o o o o o

While Penny was in Louth, Spiky Spencer – sporting a newly-acquired navy-blue baseball cap which, friends had told him, suited him "surprisingly well" – came up from Surrey to spend a few days with Alastair. This was the rearranged visit the friends had been planning for months.

"Loving the baseball cap," said Alastair.

"Why thank you, kind sir," replied Spiky. "It's my new image."

Although the Spiky hairstyle which had given Spiky his nickname as a schoolboy had yielded years ago to a more conventional style, that original nickname had real staying power – at least as far as Alastair was concerned. His view was: once Spiky Spencer, always Spiky Spencer.

Now, Spiky was looking perplexed. "What's this, Clayton?" he asked as Alastair placed two pint glasses of a near-transparent liquid down in front of his friend. It was early evening. They had just finished their tea with Vicky – beans on toast all round. In an hour they would be at the pub.

"Just to start you off, mate. Before we head off down to the Belle Vue Tavern. It's ice-cold Kopparberg Swedish pear cider. I bloody love the stuff. Er, they're not both for you, by the way. This one's mine. Our Vicky turned me onto it and I've been hooked ever since."

"Bloody hell, Clayton. It's a girl's drink, surely." But Spiky drank it enthusiastically nonetheless.

From the age of eleven, Spiky Spencer and Alastair Clayton had been friends. But it was an incident when they were aged thirteen that consolidated that friendship forever. Their class had gone swimming at the local baths. Alastair was among the poorest swimmers and always stayed in the shallow end. However, on this occasion, their teacher, Mr Cochrane, wanted to challenge the less able ones and see just what they might be capable of if they tried harder.

"Don't be frightened by what I am about to ask you to do," said Mr Cochrane, standing at the side of the pool in a navy blue tracksuit. He was in his forties, prematurely bald, an athletic type who kept himself fit, and, unlike many of his teaching colleagues, he was by no means disliked by the youngsters.

"Instead of splashing about aimlessly in the shallow end today, I'd like you to be a bit more adventurous."

An already-nervous thirteen-year-old Alastair, who would become unsettled by nothing more than the odour of chlorine even as he and the other children queued to get into the baths, let alone by the sight of the water and the dangers implied by rubber rings and polystyrene floats, was now beginning to feel real terror.

The better swimmers had now climbed out of the pool, leaving the 'deep end' clear.

"What I have in mind is this," said Mr Cochrane. "Those of

you who can swim a width, those of you who might struggle to swim a width but nevertheless can do it – at a push. I'd like to see you now swim as far as you can towards the deep end. Now, don't be worried. If you encounter difficulty, the boys stood at point A, point B, point C and point D, as well as the baths' own trained lifeguards patrolling the pool, are all in readiness, poised to help at the first sign of trouble."

Alastair gulped. He knew that Mr Cochrane had watched him three weeks before just about scramble from one side of the pool to the other, but that had been with the aid of a float, with no additional psychological pressure involved, and with the added security of two of his good friends guiding and encouraging him every inch of the way. Yes, it was true, he had completed a width, but it had been stressful and he had swallowed a lot of water en route. At the time he had not realised Mr Cochrane had been watching. It was only when the boys were getting back on the bus afterwards that his teacher had said to him: "Well done, Alastair. I saw you complete a width this week. That's a marvellous big step forward, lad. We'll make a swimmer of you yet."

Now, Alastair waited in dread, as Mr Cochrane continued with his instructions. "Okay then. I want the following six boys to line up here and we'll see how far you get."

As Mr Cochrane read out the names of the six boys, Alastair momentarily began to believe his name might not be on the list after all. Four names called out already and no mention of Alastair. Five names called out. The last name coming up . . . "and Alastair Clayton."

And Alastair knew then that no matter what was to happen to him in the years ahead, this moment would forever be remembered by him as one of the worst in his life.

Only one of the six boys who set out from the south end of the pool completed his length unaided that day. Two turned back and splashed their way to safety after thrashing about for a minute without actually making any significant progress. One was quickly rescued by a lifeguard. Another just about made it to the north end, but only with the help of an experienced swimmer. And Alastair surprised himself by getting much further than he would ever have anticipated.

He had made not insubstantial progress by employing a trick his father had told him about. Whenever trying to do something very difficult, his dad had said, try taking your mind off it by thinking of something else. It makes you less self-conscious. It helps you to stop worrying about whatever it is you are trying to achieve. And so, keeping to the rhythm of the breast stroke, Alastair had been singing in his mind one of his favourite hymns from morning assembly. Concentrating on the words and the melody of the hymn, rather than on the swimming, he pushed himself forward through the water.

All people that on earth do dwell,
Sing to the Lord with cheerful voice.
Him serve with fear, His praise forth tell;
Come ye before Him and rejoice.

It seemed to be working. The rhythm of the hymn and the rhythm of his swimming were as one.

The Lord, ye know, is God indeed;
Without our aid He did us make;
We are His folk, He doth us feed,
And for His sheep He doth us take.

O enter then His gates with praise;
Approach with joy His courts unto;
Praise, laud, and bless His Name always,
For it is seemly so to do.

But then, just a few feet away from completing his journey to the north end, he suffered a panic attack and got into trouble.

Chlorine stung his eyes. Water was in his mouth, up his nose, in his ears. He could not breathe. He thought he could see Mr Cochrane at the edge of the pool, shouting, calling to him, but Alastair could not hear any words, any sounds. He felt his entire head was full of water. Co-ordination had gone. Arms and legs powerless. He glimpsed Mr Cochrane again, his bald head shining. But nothing seemed to be happening. Why was no-one helping him?

And then Alastair felt someone grab him and lift his head high above the surface. And he knew he was going to be all right. His rescuer was Spiky Spencer, his good friend and one of the strongest swimmers in the school. He may have been short and he may not have possessed the classic physique of a top swimmer, but this boy could swim.

And, yes, right there and then – no question about it – Spiky Spencer had saved Alastair's life.

"So are we going down the pub then or what?" asked Spiky, finishing his pear cider.

"Oh, we're going down the pub all right," said Alastair. And he beamed across at his old friend with great affection.

Because, as it now occurred to him for the second time in a matter of days, and this time with even greater clarity: even in the happiest of moments there is sadness; even when we have everything, we know it cannot last.

CHAPTER SEVEN

A LITTLE FRIEND TO PLAY WITH

"Aye-up. Look here. Old Alastair has found himself a little friend to play with. He's not such a Billy-no-mates after all." It was Frank the window cleaner, arriving at the Belle Vue Tavern with his mates, John the retired baker and Paul the postman. "It's good to see you've found someone you can read The Guardian with, mate."

"Evening, fellas" said Alastair. "This is a very dear friend of mine from way back. Say hello to Spiky Spencer."

Frank, John and Paul shook hands with Spiky who told them: "Yeah. I've known Clayton here since our schooldays. I suppose you could say we have a shared history."

"Well, it's good to meet you, Spiky," said Paul. "We were starting to worry that Alastair here really was the anti-social bastard that everyone says he is. Anyway, We won't disturb you. Just having a quick one here and then we're off to the Prince for a quiz."

When the three had gone up to the bar to order their drinks, Spiky suggested to his friend that they also could go on to the quiz, but Alastair was not keen. "To be honest, I don't fancy a quiz, mate. My general knowledge is not what it should be. I'd only let you down."

"Well, if the quiz specialised in obscure pop music of the sixties and seventies, we'd walk it," said Spiky.

"That's the problem, Spike. I have a feeling the range of subjects might be a bit wider than that."

After they had each bought a round of drinks, Alastair and Spiky decided, as was customary between them, to play a game for the next round. They would have their own little two-man quiz. The first to falter would buy the drinks.

"Okay, Clayton. Here's the deal. Strange, funny, odd, quirky, obscure facts about The Beatles."

"Can't we do Donovan instead?"

"No, because you've just read a whole bloody book about Donovan and I don't know a damned thing about him. It would hardly be a level playing field."

"But how do I know that you haven't spent the last three months swotting up on the Fab Four in preparation for just this occasion?"

"You don't."

"Oh."

A couple of men were beginning a not-too-serious game of darts in the far corner, the angst-filled contralto of Amy Winehouse sang out from the jukebox, and the faint smell of disinfectant seeped out into the bar every time someone opened the door to the gents.

"But we're both Beatles fans so this seems a reasonably fair contest. Okay. I'll start with a question for you. On the Rubber Soul song, Girl, what is the mischievous, slightly naughty backing vocal."

"Oh, I *do* know this," said Alastair. "Isn't it: 'tit, tit, tit, tit, tit, tit, tit, tit, tit, tit, tit, tit, tit, tit'?"

"Correct." And Spiky knocked back his beer. "Now your turn, Clayton."

Another waft of disinfectant.

"Okay. Here's one. On Across The Universe, what is the mantra that Lennon sings at the end?"

"That's too easy, mate. It's Jai Guru Deva Om. Jai Guru Deva means 'welcome great master' or 'hail great guru' or 'get a round in, for God's sake, I'm dying for a pint'. Something like that. And 'Om' is just the vibration of the universe."

"You really have been swotting up for the last three months."

"Not a bit of it, you bugger."

"Go on then. Your turn, Spike."

Winehouse's record came to a close and the Dave Clark Five launched into Bits and Pieces. Three young women walked into the pub and both Alastair and Spiky eyed them up and down without comment, almost without thought.

"Right. Who is Billy Shears?" asked Spiky.

"There's an introduction to bandleader Billy Shears on Sgt Pepper – the one and only Billy Shears. And then Ringo goes into Little Help From My Friends. So it could be argued that Ringo was Billy Shears."

"Good enough, Clayton. Good enough."

"There's another game we could play sometime, Spike: keep naming famous Billys until we run out. Billy Shears. Billy the Kid, Billy Elliot, Billy Liar."

"Let's not forget Billy-no-mates, Clayton."

"*Ha ha*. Very funny. Then there's Backhoe Billy – that's our Vicky's ex-boyfriend. Lovely lad. I really like him. I still don't know why they ever fell out. They seemed to be so right for each other. Anyway. Excuse me a minute. Must visit the little boys' room."

In the pub toilet Alastair read a printed sign above the urinals:

"Please do not deposit your chewing gum in the urinals. It clogs up the drains and causes overflow."

And then, just underneath, someone had written in ballpoint:

"It also makes it go hard and taste funny."

Three hours later, the two old friends were walking back from the pub. Spiky, repositioning his baseball cap upon his head, was whistling Bits and Pieces, a tune which, Alastair now considered, did not readily lend itself to whistling.

Stuck to the rear windscreen of a parked car, a beaten-up old Volkswagen as it turned out, there was a familiar-looking sticker – black letters on a bright yellow diamond-shape. As Alastair now walked closer to the car, he thought: "Baby on board". But as he and his friend got closer still, he read the words: "Ex-husband in boot". There had been a time when he would have snorted with disdain at such crassness, but now he thought that if his own dear wife were to display such a sign, he wouldn't blame her. It would be no more than he deserved. He was turning out to be a rotten husband, neglectful of his lovely Penelope, unfaithful in all but deed.

Later that night, with the rest of the family in bed, and Spiky having gone up too, Alastair, out of a sense of guilt for having done so little to help around the house for such a long time, decided to (very quietly so as not to wake anyone) empty the dishwasher. He put away the glasses that, just a couple of years before, had been charged in celebration of their silver wedding anniversary, and he stopped for a moment, in the still, artificial light of the kitchen, and recalled that happy day. And, although he could not understand why this should be, it seemed to him now that it must have been some other couple who had been celebrating. How could it possibly have been he and Penny? How could it have been them on that day of joy and fun and true love, when just last week there had been such a chill between them?

"I've been waiting for you," she had said softly. The words had rolled around in his head. They had sounded loving, conciliatory, romantic.

He had turned the words over. Each word in turn.

To see if there was anything lurking underneath.

And then he had seen that there was.

"Oh, how stupid am I?" he had said, and his hands had recoiled from her body. "I understand now."

"What?" she had asked, annoyance turning her voice hard. "What does that mean? You understand now?"

"Just for a moment there, I thought you actually meant you'd been waiting for me."

Penny had sighed deeply, and glared at him, clearly upset. "Oh, for Christ's sake! What the hell is the matter with you, Alastair?"

Alastair and Penny: Their love had been shelved.
Shelved.
It had not died.
It had merely been shelved.
That is how it felt to Alastair at least.

They had grown apart somehow. Neither of them would have been able to explain it. It was just "one of those things".

Over a period of many weeks, an almost unexpressed yet growing dislike of one another had gently transformed itself into indifference. Conversation was kept to a minimum. Affection had been put on hold. Meanwhile, their daughter quietly prayed to no god in particular that it would all come right in the end.

When he was not absorbed in his uninspiring yet nonetheless challenging work at the estate agents, Alastair filled his head with inconsequential musings. For instance, when down at the Belle Vue Tavern alone, he would spend an almost disturbing amount of time trying to guess which song would next pop up on the jukebox. His guess was never correct, but he enjoyed the game. And sometimes he would scribble across the top of his Guardian the tunes and artists that were played that evening. He loved the randomness of the jukebox. Different customers with utterly different tastes would come in and make their selections and you would get Creedence Clearwater Revival followed by Oasis followed by The Eagles; The Searchers followed by Muse followed by Stealers Wheel; Gerry and the Pacemakers followed by Blur followed by Lindisfarne.

And somewhere in a corner of his mind he knew that all this nonsense – writing down the names of songs, trying the guess the next selection – was part of some sort of avoidance technique.

However, when a little drunk, when a little tired, he found he could sometimes avoid the matter in hand no longer. He thought about Penelope and a tear would dribble down the side of his nose. It was not so much that he did not want to save his marriage; more that he felt he did not have the means or the strength or the energy to save it. It was like his heart was not really in it. He felt that, at least for the moment, he was beyond help, beyond hope, like a moth caught up in a spider's web.

Alastair could hear his mother, forty years earlier, bitterness ringing in her voice, almost screaming at his father:

"What happened to the man I married?

"Where did he go to?

"He was so kind and considerate.

"He was so nice to be with."

And then, with tears in her eyes: *"He was so loving. What happened to him?*

"Can you tell me?

"Can you tell me?"

And now Alastair wondered if he was going the same way as his dad – turning into a useless husband, a husband with nothing more to give.

Alastair the Useless.

Alastair the Hopeless.

Alastair the Spent.

He occasionally wondered exactly when the rot had begun to set in. Unlike during the early years of their marriage, they now rarely went to the theatre or the cinema or the pub together. But when had that change come about? And, in more mundane ways too, he and Penny were leading separate lives. They would even get dressed in separate rooms at different times. His clothes in readiness for the morning he would place in the spare room so that the sound of him getting dressed would not disturb Penelope. This he had started to do some time ago for those mornings when Penny was not going to work or when his start time was earlier than hers. But eventually it had become such a habit that he now dressed in the spare room every morning.

Oh, Penny. Oh, Penny.

What happened?

In some ways he is, he thinks to himself now, often more loving towards his passed-away parents. More loving towards them (or their spirits) than to his still-flesh-and-blood wife. Sometimes, in the middle of a shave or while sitting in the garden or while flicking around the television channels or while idly washing up a mug that has somehow missed the dishwasher, he will, for a nanosecond, less than a nanosecond, think his long-dead parents still tread this mortal coil. In a daydream state he will fleetingly forget that they are dead. His reality will have shifted – past and present merging as milk and coffee merge in a latte. But then before he reaches what would have been his next logical thought – *'must give them a call, must go round and see them'* – he will realise his silly error and he will smile to himself. "Love you, Mum. Love you, Dad," he will tell the shaving mirror or the garden or the television or the mug he is washing in the sink.

Vicky awoke from a disturbingly vivid dream one Sunday morning and as she came round she could remember every detail. She had been Laurey in Oklahoma! except that, thinking about it now, she had been every bit as beautiful as Shirley Jones had been playing Laurey in the famous film version. She had sung Out Of My Dreams against a stunning Oklahoma sky. The lighting and backdrop were perfect. Her singing was exquisite. She danced a long and intimate dance with a man, a dance far longer and far more intimate than the one she was required to perform in the Pigeons' production. The man was Curly, the handsome cowboy, played by Connor. But, in the dream, the personas of Curly and Connor were indistinguishable. They were one and the same person.

It is clear for all to see: Curly and Laurey are in love with each other. The audience is urging their love to succeed.

But then, in Vicky's dream, just as in the intoxicating dream sequence in the Rodgers and Hammerstein musical, Jud, the

hired ranch hand who is also in love with Laurey, appears with an ensemble of garish good-time girls; sexy saloon women in fancy low-cut dresses that show off their figures, dresses of purple and emerald and turquoise and pink. A honky-tonk piano plays in the background.
There is something not quite right here.
Jud is angry, jealous, unstable. This dream is turning into a nightmare.
Then the Laurey-Vicky character suddenly realises something. The bad guy in this story, Jud, the one who stands between Laurey and Curly, is actually Backhoe Billy.
Laurey stares into the face of Jud. Staring back at her is the face of Billy.
"Please go away, Billy, and leave Curly and I in peace so we can marry and live happily ever after," she pleads. "I don't want anyone to get hurt."
But there is nothing she can do to prevent the melodrama playing out. The skies darken. The music becomes menacing.
There is a ferocious fight between Jud and Curly. The prize for the winner will be Laurey.
A terrible storm rages all about and then Jud kills Curly with his bare hands. Then the mad, bad Jud turns to Laurey. He picks her up roughly and carries her off. Connor lies dead. Backhoe Billy, a destroyer of happiness, is victorious.

February trudged on past without drama of any kind in the Clayton household. It was a dull month, uneventful, and more than a little depressing. But drama of one kind at least was promised by the arrival of March. The Pigeons' production of Oklahoma! was about to open. Olivia was getting ready to travel across from Louth to be with her daughter, son-in-law and grand-daughter in their handsome red brick house in South Hermitage. Her precious Vicky was to star in the role of Laurey Williams, and Olivia was not going to miss that for the world.

A week before the curtain was due to go up on Oklahoma!, Olivia rang from Louth. Vicky picked up the phone.

"Oh, hi Grandma. How's you?"

"I'm fine, my dear. And how's my favourite grand-daughter?"

"You mean your *only* grand-daughter."

"Don't be so pedantic. All right are you?"

"Couldn't be better."

"And how's your love life?"

"Grandma! You can't ask me that?"

"And why not?"

"You just can't. That's all."

"Still seeing that bloke who's playing Curly in the play?"

Vicky's mind shot back to that first kiss in the layby. There had been many kisses since then, but this was not something she wished to go into detail about with her grandmother – nor anyone else for that matter.

Olivia asked the question again. "Have you gone deaf, child? Are you still seeing the bloke who plays Curly?"

"Well. Still seeing him in so far as we rehearse together. Yeah. But still seeing him as in 'romance' between us. Not quite. We're really not quite there yet.

This was what Vicky's mum and dad would have called 'a little white lie'. The truth was that Vicky and Connor were definitely 'in a relationship' now, albeit an at times confusing one for Vicky.

She continued with this disingenuous tale, telling Olivia: "That's not to say it couldn't happen. There is a chance it just might. We're kinda dancing around the notion, if you know what I mean. But the breakthrough is yet to come. We are lovers on stage only. Seeing as you insist on knowing."

"Don't you get to kiss him on stage?"

"Grandma. A stage kiss is not the same as a real kiss. And, truth be told, there is precious little kissing in this production. Actually, no kissing at all. Nestling up to one another. Looking into each other's eyes adoringly. Yeah. All that. But no actual kissing."

"Honestly, Vick. I don't understand you youngsters at all. I thought we had gone through the Permissive Society decades ago. If you fancy the chap, just grab hold of him and tell him."

Vicky's chat with her grandmother was interrupted as Penelope called: "Vick! Something has arrived for you." It was a large and colourful bouquet being delivered by a man at the front door, a man from a florists. While Vicky took receipt of the flowers, Penny took the phone and spoke to Olivia. "Someone's sent her some lovely flowers," said Penny.

"Oh. I wonder if it's Curly."

"You mean Connor, mother. Curly is the character he plays."

"I know that. How many times do you think I've watched Oklahoma? – it's one of my favourites."

But it turned out the flowers were not from Connor. They were from Backhoe Billy; his somewhat belated phase two of his 'Get Back With Vicky' campaign.

The message attached read:

Vicky,
I still love you, my sweetheart.
Please let's try again.
Give me a call.
Billy

Without any great enthusiasm, Vicky placed the flowers in the biggest vase she could find and then went upstairs and tucked the little card bearing the message into a drawer in her dressing table.

She glanced quickly at some other words now, the words she had written beneath her dressing table mirror – words written months before, put together in the brightly coloured Early Learning Centre magnetic letters she had had one Christmas when she was a toddler, a message that was part 'note to self', part cry for help:

LOOKIN FOR LOVE

She had never been able to find the letter 'g' to complete

the word 'looking'.

When she came back downstairs, she said under her breath: "Don't throw bouquets at me" – taking a line from a song in Oklahoma!.

"Ah, that's a lovely song, that," said Penelope.

"Oh, sorry. I didn't realise you were in earshot. I was just thinking aloud."

"Well, I didn't mean to eavesdrop on your thinking aloud. Great song though. 'People Will Say We're In Love'. That's the song that those words come from, isn't it? Don't throw bouquets at me? Then something about not pleasing my folks too much because people will say we're in love. But surely, that song is sung by Laurey to Curly, the love of her life?"

"And your point is?"

"Well that very vivid dream you had . . . "

"Oh God. Did I actually tell you about that stupid dream, Mum?"

"You did."

"Oh bugger."

"Anyway. The point I'm trying to make is that, in your dream, the bad guy – Jud – was Backhoe Billy. But it isn't Jud that Laurey pleads with: Don't throw bouquets at me. It's Curly, the good guy, the nice cowboy who sings 'Oh What A Beautiful Morning'. So therefore it figures that, if we are to interpret your dream in the light of actual events which have just taken place, Backhoe Billy isn't the bad guy at all. He's actually the good guy. Backhoe Billy is the one who is throwing bouquets at you, not Connor. Backhoe Billy, therefore, might I humbly suggest, is the one you are destined to be with. The one you truly love."

"Bloody hell, Mum. I do hope you're not thinking about giving up teaching in favour of psychiatry."

"Oh, please yourself." And her mum walked off to the kitchen to make a cup of tea.

Whenever, over the next few days, either of her parents tried to talk to her about the bouquet or about Billy, Vicky would say sharply: "I really don't want to discuss it." And that would be that.

One chilly Monday evening, Penelope was passing by her daughter's bedroom and called: "You okay, Love?"

"Yeah. I'm fine, Mum," came the reply. "You can come in and have a chat if you like. . . providing we don't talk about Billy and the flowers."

They talked instead about less controversial topics: perfume, clothes, Oklahoma! and the current crop of films on at the cinema. Then, Penelope noticed her daughter had a Facebook page up on her computer. "Just for a bit of fun, Vick. Show me how this thing works. How easy is it to get in touch with old friends that you've lost contact with?"

"Here. Let me show you," said Vicky.

"Hang on a minute. I'll get a glass of wine. Do you want one?"

"That would be nice." It was not too often that Vicky spent time like this with her mother.

It was like having a little friend to play with.

CHAPTER EIGHT

TRIUMPH AT THE VILLAGE HALL

"What did you want to see us about?" asked Rachael, slowly stirring her tall latte with the long spoon provided. She looked idly out of the window, watching the people in the street below – in and out of the market hall with shopping bags and pushchairs.

"What makes you think it was anything in particular?" asked Vicky, shooting glances from Rachael to Zoe, Zoe to Rachael, and back again.

"Oh, come on, Vick. We all know we've been pals a long time," said Rachael, "but, honestly, when was the last time just the three of us got together like this? I mean, we're all pals, yes, of course we are. But we normally get together with the gang in an evening. This is slightly unusual. Afternoon coffees. I mean – have we ever done this before? It feels like a business meeting."

"Always one to call a spade a spade," said Vicky, cutting her Danish pastry into manageable pieces.

Zoe, like a gentle referee, smiled at her two friends. And then she said: "Oh, come on, you two. Play nicely."

Rachael had already been stung into an apology and said: "Oh, I'm sorry, Vick. Am I being blunt again?" And her tone was completely sincere which in turn made Vicky feel embarrassed. Rachael continued: "I must try harder not to be so forthright. It is a failing in me, I know. I'm always blurting things out, things which are better left unsaid."

"I'm saying nothing," said Zoe, and sipped her hot chocolate.

"Okay. Let's start again," said Vicky. "I asked you to meet me here because firstly I *do* regard you both as very good friends and not just fairweather pals. We've all known each other a good while. We understand one another, I think. We should see each other more often. You're good company and I'm really sorry we don't see more of each other. And secondly, and now it's my time to be blunt, I do have an agenda, actually, I'm a little embarrassed to admit. You see, I asked you both here because you, Zoe dear, happen to be my boyfriend's sister, and you, Rachael sweetie, have met him a fair few times, and I could really do with some information, some insight into Connor."

They were on the first floor of Ashley's restaurant and, it being a quiet day in town, they had the room to themselves.

"Oh, so you are definitely boyfriend and girlfriend?" asked Rachael. "I wasn't quite sure."

"Neither was I for a long time," said Vicky, and she chuckled nervously to herself. "In fact, I'm still not entirely convinced even now."

"Oh. How come?" asked Rachael, pushing a tumbling lock of her silky black hair back over one ear.

Vicky looked into her friend's big dark eyes. It was then that she thought perhaps the reason she had not readily invited Rachael out for a chat like this for such a long time, the reason why she – Vicky – had always felt more comfortable in the 'larger group environment' offered by her little gang of friends, was actually to do with Rachael's obvious beauty. Now, Zoe – the third member of this trio – was attractive too, but Rachael was a stunner – she knew it, everyone knew it. Stupid, Vicky thought now, but she had always been a little intimidated by Rachael's good looks. She had always felt inferior in her company. And she knew full well that, whenever she and Rachael were being eyed up by men, it was always Rachael who had really caught their eye. She knew that even if she applied make-up the way in which Rachael did, even if she spent as much money on her hair as Rachael did, this was a competition that would only ever have one clear winner. And she guessed their mutual friend, Zoe, would surely have felt much the same way about the situation.

Vicky pushed a piece of Danish pastry around her plate.

Zoe was next to speak: "Well, we're waiting. How come you still have doubts about your relationship with my brother? We're intrigued, aren't we, Rach?"

"Mmmm. Well now. What can I tell you? I find him mysterious, enigmatic. He plays his cards very close to his chest. He doesn't give much away about himself. I think I know where I stand, but then I don't. And even after all these months of rehearsing Oklahoma! together, I honestly don't think I know him very well at all? Is any of this ringing any bells with you."

"Of course it is. He's always been like that," said Zoe. "I can't honestly say I know him very well – and we grew up together, for heaven's sake."

"Oh, well that's reassuring at least. It's not just me who finds him slightly odd."

"Have you . . . ?"

"I know what you're asking, Zoe, and I'm a little bit shocked at your audacity, quite frankly, my dear, but believe me, we are nothing like at that stage. We've kissed and cuddled a bit, you know, but . . ."

"Okay, okay. I'm sorry. I don't actually need the detail, y'know? Just trying to work out what kind of a relationship the two of you have."

"And there you go, you see. Because, clearly, this is not something he ever discusses with you, I take it. He doesn't talk about me to you, Zoe? He doesn't give you any clues as to how we're doing?"

"Well, no. And to be fair, Vick, it's not the kind of thing I would ask him about really. You know what I mean? We talk about fairly superficial stuff, but never anything too serious. I think that's pretty normal. Brothers and sisters rarely share intimate secrets. At least, we never have."

"Yeah. I think I get that."

"I'm not sure I'm being a great deal of help to you."

Vicky did not answer immediately and popped another piece of Danish pastry in her mouth. And then, after a moment, she said: "Well. Can either of you tell me anything about his hobbies and interests? His history. His friends. He just never tells me anything. He can be exasperating. It's like trying to get blood out of a stone."

"Friends? Mmmmm. Well he has an old school mate he sometimes goes to see up in Manchester."

"You see. I never knew that. Why has he never mentioned that to me?"

"I've no idea."

"So who is this friend in Manchester?"

While Rachael now drank the last sip of her latte, Zoe said: "I think his name's Sam. Couple of times a year he'll say he's going to be away at the weekend because he's off up north to see Sam. Think they used to play football together when they were at school. Unless I'm getting confused with someone else. But no, pretty sure it's Sam. He's an old pal and Connor has kept in touch with him over the years. Rather nice really."

"And that's it?"

"Well, he's got his friends at the operatic society. He likes Jake."

"Ah, now, I know Jake. He's the soundman for the Pigeons. He's all right. I like him. And he's the one who came out in his Range Rover that very first night that Connor and I were going out to Acton Virgil and I had no idea where we were going because he insisted on keeping it a secret. Jake brought us a can of fuel for the car because we'd run out of petrol. He's a good guy."

"Well, there you go. Jake is a mate of his. Couple of others in the Pigeons he's quite pally with, I think. And, as I say, this Sam chappie in Manchester. But that's about it on the friends front."

"Hobbies, interests, background, history?"

"As you know, he loves his musicals. Loves Rodgers and Hammerstein. Loves Shrewsbury."

"Ah, now there's something. One of the very first things he ever asked me, and I thought it was slightly odd at the time, was 'Do you love Shrewsbury?' He asked me that that very first time we met, at the garden party last year. Slightly strange question, I thought."

"Okay. Now, I can actually help you with this one," said Zoe, for the first time looking genuinely engaged with the subject under discussion. "I might be able to give you, as you would say, a little insight into this."

"Do tell."

And even Rachael, who for a moment had looked a little distracted, staring out of the window, now began to look interested again.

"Okay. It's like this. His last two girlfriends . . ."

"Oh, that's good as well. He has *had* other girlfriends. So he's not gay, then?"

"What? You thought he was gay?"

"Well, it wouldn't have surprised me. Y'know. Rodgers and Hammerstein, for heaven's sake? How many young blokes like Rodgers and Hammerstein in this day and age . . . unless they're gay of course. And now I hear about a mysterious man-friend he's never mentioned to me, living up in Manchester. He goes to visit him from time to time. Know what I mean?"

"Oh, honestly, Vick. No, I think I can safely say my brother is not gay. He's had at least two serious girlfriends in the past couple of years."

"Fair enough. You were saying . . ."

"Yes. I was saying his last two girlfriends told me that, very early on, Connor had asked that exact question."

"Sorry. What exact question? I'm losing my way now."

"The one about Shrewsbury. 'Do you love Shrewsbury?'. He had asked each of them that early on in their, well, period of going out together. And he asked you that very same question on the very first night he met you."

"Yeah."

"Yeah."

"But what possible significance might that have?"

"Do you know what, Vick? I have absolutely no idea."

"Great."

Zoe made a face which said: "I know. I'm hopeless, aren't I?"

Vicky smiled and slowly shook her head.

Rachael piped up: "He's a real man of mystery, Connor, isn't he? And I'm sorry, Vick, but I really don't know that much about him at all. Apart from the fact that he tells some pretty awful jokes. He once told me this one about a family of balloons."

"Yes. I know. He told me that one as well."

They could hear the friendly laughter of the waitresses downstairs, and the sounds of the clearing of tables and the preparation of fresh orders, the comforting clink of plate upon plate, cup upon saucer. Vicky recovered a stray piece of icing which had broken away from her Danish pastry. She balanced it on the tip of her forefinger and popped it in her mouth. For a moment, she was a little girl again, sitting with her mum and dad in some tiny cafe in Much Wenlock or Church Stretton, the promise of a souvenir badge on the horizon.

They paid the bill, stepped outside into the afternoon sunshine, and walked, the three of them together like the good friends that they were, towards Marks & Spencer.

"So what happened to these girlfriends then?" asked Vicky.

"Oh, well the first one dumped Connor. I think she just found someone else, someone she was more suited to, y'know? These things happen."

"All's fair in love and war," said Vicky.

"Exactly. And the other one was determined to go and live in Australia. Well, of course, Connor is a home-lovin' boy. He wouldn't have wanted to live in Australia."

"Not even for love?"

"Oh, I don't think it was ever quite that serious. Not serious enough to emigrate for."

"I see."

"I shouldn't worry about it, Vick."

"God, life's a mess though, isn't it? You want things to run smoothly. They rarely do. You want everything to fit nicely into place. It doesn't. Life's just a big old mess." And then, thinking about the cry-for-help message on her dressing table back home – LOOKIN FOR LOVE – she added: "You never do find the 'g'."

"Blimey, Vick!" said Rachael. "Finding the 'g'? Where did that come from? You saucy thing."

"Oh, Rach. For God's sake. I'm not talking about the G-spot. Bloody hell. I'm talking about a missing Early Learning Centre magnetic letter. For years, I haven't been able to find the letter 'g'. Sorry. I keep forgetting that some people actually *have* a sex life."

Looking utterly puzzled, Rachael said: "Er . . . well, you guys. Shall we see what M&S has to offer?"

"Why not?" said Zoe, and the three of them marched into the store in search of retail therapy.

Monday morning again and Alastair had had his Weetabix and his cranberry juice and his Omega 3 tablet and was heading off to the offices of Penfold, Carroll and Walsh. On the car CD player was a vintage album by his favourite 1970s folk-rockers, Paper Bubble. As he drove along Town Walls, past the Roman Catholic cathedral, he attempted to squirt screenwash at his dirty windscreen, but he had run out. "Bloody hell," he said to himself.

He spent the first two hours of his working day making phone calls and messing about with blunt pencils, trying to decide whether it was worth sharpening them as opposed to simply getting some new ones.

At lunchtime he again found himself sharing a table with

Beth at Poppy's restaurant.

"Have you made any plans for a holiday this year?" she asked.

"It's only March, Beth. We tend to leave things til later in the year and then have a couple of breaks at the seaside. Vicky doesn't come with us anymore. She's all grown up and likes to do her own thing. So it's just me and Penny left to please ourselves."

"That's nice."

"Yeah. It is. It is."

"Well, I have a bit of a plan forming." she said.

"Oh yeah? What's that then?" he asked, at once worried and excited that Beth's plan might somehow involve him.

"I have a younger sister. She's married. They have two kids, a boy and a girl. They're adorable. Really adorable, actually. And they have a chalet near Aberystwyth. They actually own their own holiday chalet. Quite well off, as you can imagine. And it's quite big, this chalet. So they've invited me to join them for a fortnight's holiday in May. I think they feel a bit sorry for me – the spinster sister who can't find love."

Alastair put down his cup of coffee and looked into Beth's eyes. He took her hand and said: "Oh Beth. Don't say things like that. You'll find love. You will. You're bloody gorgeous." Where was this boldness coming from?, he asked himself. The conversation was becoming too intimate. He would have to try to change the subject, cool things down.

"You're very kind, Al, but I think I'm the kind of woman who scares men away somehow. They like me well enough for a while, but then they decide they don't want to commit. Next thing you know, they've gone."

"Beth dearest. If I wasn't already married . . . " So much for cooling things down, he told himself. Could he not show some restraint here? "But I am married. Happily married. And that's how it is, I'm afraid."

o o o o o o

Every seat was taken at Acton Virgil village hall. Indeed, some optimistic people who turned up to the venue without having already booked a ticket had to be turned away, and the Pigeons had decided to add an extra night to the production's run, such was its popularity. This was surely in some part due to the publicity given to the production in the run-up to opening night. Connor, using his beloved Pentax K-5 digital SLR, had taken some fine photographs of the cast at dress rehearsals and three of these had been published alongside a feature article in the Shrewsbury Chronicle.

The buzz of conversation from the audience now died away as the lights dimmed. The curtains opened to reveal Connor as Curly McLain in cowboy hat, blue jeans, silver-buckled belt, rusty-orange shirt, blue neckerchief, exactly like Gordon MacRae in the film version. However, not having a Hollywood-sized budget behind this production, Connor was bobbing gently upon a wooden horse, surrounded by a field of cardboard corn, against a background of a brilliant sky of blue paint. Connor delivered 'Oh What a Beautiful Morning' to the enchanted audience and received rapturous applause. From that moment on, everyone associated with the Pigeons knew it was going to be a great night.

Later in the performance, throughout the entire four-and-a-half minutes of the seductive duet, 'People Will Say We're In Love', Connor and Vicky could not keep their eyes off each other, and although this is exactly what Rodgers and Hammerstein intended for Curly and Laurey during the singing of this song, the Acton Virgil audience sensed this was more than mere acting. Their suspicions were confirmed when Connor and Vicky ended the song with a long, lingering kiss. In the movie version, Gordon MacRae and Shirley Jones simply snuggle up cheek-to-cheek. There is no kiss. Nor had Connor and Vicky kissed during rehearsals of the song. This had not been planned.

Lost in that kiss, it took Connor and Vicky a moment to realise the audience was on its feet for a standing ovation.

Upon realisation, the couple smiled sheepishly at the crowd and acknowledged the applause with a wave.

At the back of the hall, a young man who was immeasurably more interested in football than he was in the musical theatre, but who had come to see the girl he loved starring in Oklahoma!, quietly left the building.

"Game over," he said to himself, the fresh air hitting him full-on as the doors shut behind him. And an owl in the nearby woods seemed to mock him with its call.

Driving home later that night, Connor and Vicky knew that, for them, the evening had been a triumph in more ways than one.

CHAPTER NINE

SHREWSBURY STATION

It was the first week of May. Beth was away on holiday with her sister, brother-in-law, nephew and niece at the chalet in Aberystwyth. Meanwhile, life at the red brick house in South Hermitage was plodding along without excitement. Penny had decided that Alastair had simply become more withdrawn since the car crash – nine months ago now – and had perhaps become old before his time. She was not especially upset by this and was more or less prepared to live with the situation. Alastair, on the other hand, felt that Penny had deliberately built a wall between the two of them. His frustration centred around his own inability to break down that wall.

And office life for Alastair – office life without Beth around – had been almost unbearably dull. It had been only a few days, but he had been taken aback at just how much he had missed her.

He had especially missed their lunchtimes together at Poppy's. He had missed her perfume, her raunchy hairstyle, the gentle bounce of her bosom buttoned into a tight blouse. He had missed also her conversation and her friendship and the closeness that they had.

The only changes at the office since the start of the new year had been the replacement of the Birds of The British Isles calendar with one entitled Trees of The British Isles, and the replacement of his old chipped Batman mug with a Beatles mug his daughter had bought him ("I couldn't find a Donovan one," she had teased, "nor a Paper Bubble one."). The mug, which had been wrapped in paper patterned with paw prints, had been handed to him by Vicky on Christmas morning, but had been, of course, his present "from Chesterton". Alastair had put his pens and pencils in his new mug rather than use it for drinks as, when it came to tea or coffee, the staff of Penfold, Carroll and Walsh tended to make do with the little plastic cups from the vending machine. His old chipped Batman mug had ended up stuffed into the bottom drawer of his desk because this too had been a present from his daughter (or Chesterton) and he could not bear to part with it.

The days dragged by. But there was a thrill in store for the disillusioned Shrewsbury estate agent with the seemingly disinterested wife.

Although Beth had told her sister that she would stay the whole fortnight with them at the chalet, by the end of the first week she had made up her mind to return to Shrewsbury a few days earlier than the others, giving the family some time to themselves without 'Auntie Beth' getting in the way. She would go back the Wednesday of the second week.

r u missing me?

Alastair was a little shocked at how exciting he had found Beth's text. How could four words – well, two words and two letters to be precise – generate within him such yearning? He was keen to respond.

missing u like crazy

He pressed 'send' without a thought.

She replied she was coming home Wednesday evening.
He tapped in:

> thank god

Beth's next text made his heart beat faster:

> y dont u meet me?

He tapped in:

> When? Where?

Back came:

> Wednesday. Shrewsbury Station just after 6

Done.
The arrangement was made.
But a little white lie was needed.
He would tell his wife that he was showing a client around a property and he would probably be out for a few hours. He might also add that he would then be meeting a couple of mates in the pub later. She would accept that.

Connor had gone to Manchester for a few days to spend time with his old school pal. He would be heading back to Shropshire on the Wednesday. By Vicky's reckoning his train would arrive back in Shrewsbury around ten past six. She could surprise him. They could meet up and go for a drink together in town. Vicky was looking forward to it. She imagined herself and Connor sipping wine in an intimate bar, making plans for the coming weeks, perhaps – in a softly lit corner – 'canoodling' as her grandma would have called it.
She and Connor had been going steady now for about three

months, she was suddenly enjoying telling people. She had even abandoned the 'little white lies' and confessed to her grandmother that her 'favourite grandaughter' and Curly from Oklahoma! were now an item. And, if you were to bolt on to that figure of three months the period of friendship prior to their relationship becoming 'romantic', you might even say they had been going steady for nine months – although even Vicky would have had to admit that that was a rather fanciful way of looking at things.

Wednesday afternoon was bathed in bright sunshine. Having finished her shift at Next, Vicky had popped home for a quick shower and change of clothes and then walked into town. She always enjoyed the exercise.

She had taken in with relish the familiar old shop fronts of Coleham, the view of the river from the Greyfriars Bridge, the church on the river's bend, the weeping willows, the swans. It was – and she almost said it out loud – a fine day.

She marched into the railway station foyer feeling like the star of a romantic movie about to throw herself into the arms of her man. On the platform, the air was still. The station was quiet. She popped a lemon bon-bon into her mouth and it fizzed deliciously. Even though she was wearing a watch, she glanced up at the big clock overhanging the platform – a seemingly ancient clock which was surely there more for decoration than for practical use in this digital age. She was more than twenty minutes early.

Soon others began to gather on the platform and also on Platform 3 across the lines. Not all of these people were passengers; many of them – judging by their lack of luggage – had come to meet and greet loved ones just as she had.

At the precise moment that Vicky popped a second lemon bon-bon in her mouth, Alastair pulled into the station car park oblivious to the fact that his daughter had arrived at the station just minutes before.

He pondered over whether he should stay in the car or go up onto the platform. He could not decide. Butterflies, people called it. When your innards were all knotted up with nerves, when you longed for something to be over and done with, when the worry felt like an illness that was twisting at your stomach, making a cross-stitch of your intestines.

He knew full well that this was madness, but it was a madness over which he seemed to have no control.

No. It would be nicer to meet her on the platform. Nicer? *Nicer?* He almost laughed at the idea that there was anything remotely "nice" about this situation. What's nice about deceitfulness? What's nice about betrayal? What's nice about cheating on your wife?

Alastair noticed the stern-faced gargoyles on the station's gothic-style frontage. They seemed to be looking down at him in judgement. They seemed to be asking: "Is this what you really want to do?"

For a moment, he felt nauseous. And in the midst of that nausea he experienced another one of his flashbacks to his childhood.

One day, when he was a boy, he now recalled, he had gone into his bedroom in the middle of the afternoon to play with his train set. The loop of track and the couple of simple sidings could not have been dignified with the term "model railway layout" – not like the miniature village Alastair's dad had taken him to see once at the home of a man who lived near the Prince of Wales. No. That man had most decidedly had a fully-fledged model railway layout. Young Alastair's set-up was a mere train set. But on this particular afternoon, the twelve-year-old Alastair had been startled to find a blackbird that had flown in through the open window and was now sitting right in the middle of the train set.

The bird looked like it had been stunned. It would occasionally move its head slightly, but otherwise hardly moved at all. It looked utterly lost as if it had flown through a portal into another universe and was having trouble coming to terms with its alien surroundings. And now here was the adult Alastair, as utterly lost as that blackbird had been, having trouble coming to terms with his alien surroundings.

He had no recollection of walking up the steps to Platform

5 and yet, as if in a dream, he found himself there. The train was not due for another quarter of an hour. Should he stand still or would he be less conspicuous if he walked a few yards along the platform and back again?

For a few minutes he stood with his back against the brick wall of the station restaurant. He looked dead ahead, still wondering what exactly he hoped to achieve by coming to the station in the first place. Then he started walking down the platform, hoping he would not see anyone he knew. Eventually he sat on a bench, searching his pockets for a sweet to chew. He found none. After another five minutes, realising he still had plenty of time before the train came in, he got up and walked into the restaurant, finding a corner table. He wished he had a newspaper to flap through. That, at least, would have made him feel less conspicuous. He bought himself a coffee, but decided against buying a newspaper so late in the day. Sitting back down, he stirred his drink. He would never normally stir his drink like this. But he stirred and he stirred.

"Dad? What on earth are you doing here?"

Alastair looked up at his daughter with an expression which seemed to move slowly from extreme puzzlement to pleasant surprise and then back to extreme puzzlement. He knew that he ought to be responding to his daughter's question, that he ought to be at least attempting to string a sentence together, but the words would not come. He instinctively rose to his feet and asked Vicky: "Would you like a coffee?"

"Er . . . well, I wouldn't say no – but, Dad, you still haven't answered my question. Are you all right? You look worried."

"No, no, no, not at all. I'm perfectly all right. Please. Let me get you a coffee and I'll tell you all about it. Er . . . why are you here anyway, darling?"

"I'm meeting Connor. He's on his way back from Manchester. You know, he sometimes goes up there to spend a bit of time with an old school pal. I just thought I would come and meet him."

"Oh, of course. Of course. Listen. You just sit there a minute. I'll get you that drink."

Alastair thought that going up to the counter to buy his daughter a coffee would at least give him a moment to think of something to tell her, to think of some story other than "I'm here to meet a woman and to take her for a drink and . . . well, who knows where that might lead?" He would have to think quickly, and thinking quickly was not really his forte.

As he returned to the table with his daughter's coffee, Alastair had decided he would tell only the smallest of lies. In fact, it was really not a lie at all. He would tell her he was meeting a work colleague – which was true. He would have to follow this up by saying something like: "We're having to thrash out the details of a new scheme for streamlining systems in the office and there was never going to be enough time at work to do it and so . . . "

Oh but wait. Had he not already told his wife that he was having to show a property to a prospective client? If Penny and Vicky ever discussed any of this (and of course they would) their stories would have to match up.

Alastair decided to stick to the prospective client story. But before he could show that person the property they were interested in, he was meeting up with a colleague who was an expert on that particular type of house. Yes, that was it.

But just as he was honing his story to perfection, Alastair – arriving back at the table with his daughter's coffee – watched the restaurant door swing open and came face to face with his second shock of the evening. He stared in utter disbelief as his wife walked into the room.

Penny immediately spotted her husband and her daughter and said: "Good grief! What are you two doing here?"

Once again Alastair was speechless, and – while staring at his wife – completely failed to notice a man in a navy blue baseball cap who had followed Penny into the restaurant and who now quietly watched the scene before him unfold.

Eventually, a few lame words came to the normally eloquent Alastair. "Hello Penny," he said. "I'm just having a coffee with Vicky here who has come to meet Connor."

"Oh, yes, that's right," said Penelope. "Connor's been to

Manchester for a few days, hasn't he? I'd forgotten about that. But why are you here as well, Alastair?"

He now vaguely recalled having spun a yarn to Penny, something about meeting a client, but the details of that lie were now shrouded in mist and he was getting tired of having to make things up. For a second, he thought about pretending to faint or pretending to have a heart attack, just so that he would not have to say anything. Just so he would not have to lie to both his wife and his daughter, the two people he loved most in the world. He felt like the floor of the restaurant had turned to quicksand and was consuming him, indeed he wished with all his heart that it *would* consume him to get him out of this predicament.

"Well?" asked Penny. And although she remembered perfectly well the story he had given her about having to meet a client on Wednesday evening, she had not for a second believed it and nor did she believe it now. She was not going to help him out. She was enjoying watching him squirm.

Alastair began stirring his coffee again.

"Well?" repeated Penny.

And just then, Alastair heard what he momentarily took to be the voice of God. It was a voice that came out of nowhere. It was a voice with an answer.

"Penny, I hope you don't mind, but I persuaded dear old Alastair, through the magic of texting, to meet me tonight so that we could go out together, have several pints – and possibly even a whisky or two – and put this crazy old world to rights before those pesky politicians get the chance to muck it all up again."

It was Spiky Spencer – now removing his baseball cap in deference to the ladies. And he had not finished speaking. "I realise it's all a bit last-minute. Terribly sudden. Should have let you know, really. Terribly rude of me. But I've got a sleeping bag with me so if I could crash at your place afterwards, Penny, I promise I won't be any trouble."

Alastair remained speechless.

Penny – clearly taken aback and more than a little puzzled –

glanced at her husband, then at Vicky, then returned to Spiky. Penelope's first thought was that it had been a mere three months since Spiky's last visit – and now here he was again. And this being a man who one would normally see rarely from one year to the next. But she quickly dismissed this thought and said: "Er . . . no, that's absolutely fine, Spiky. You know you're always welcome."

"I know we should have flagged it up with you sooner. It was just that the idea came to me in a flash while I was on the train. I was actually on my way to Wales to do some serious walking and take some photographs. That's what I'm into these days – hill-walking and photography. But I've got plenty of time. I'm off for two whole weeks. I can carry on with my journey tomorrow. It really doesn't matter to me. And so I just sent a text to old Alastair here – spontaneous like, spur of the moment – and arranged a get-together this very evening."

Alastair, even now, was speechless, proving, as if proof were needed, that quick thinking was definitely, unquestionably, not his forte.

Penny said it would be a pleasure to put a roof over the head of their dear old friend, Spiky Spencer. She went on to explain that she, just like her daughter and her husband, was on the station to meet someone. She was supposed to be meeting and greeting Professor Franzen, coming in from Church Stretton, to deliver a lecture to the Literary and Philosophical Society on the life of Dylan Thomas. His train was due in soon. The meeting did not start until 8pm so she was going to take Professor Franzen for a bite to eat and then drive him to the meeting. "He doesn't drive himself, you see. So he needed someone to pick him up from the station and then drop him back at the station after the meeting. So . . . I *am* that person!"

"So let me get this right," said Spiky. "All three members of the same family are on the railway station at exactly the same time in order to meet three other people – and none of you knew that the other two members of the family were going to be here."

"So it would seem," said Alastair, nervously looking around

in anticipation of Beth showing up and blowing his heaven-sent Spiky Spencer alibi out of the water. He also wondered why his friend had deemed it necessary to come out with this torrent of lies about texting and arranging a get-together. Had it really been so obvious to Spiky that a lifeline had been called for?

"Anyway, I'd better get out onto the platform else I'll miss Connor," said Vicky.

"Yeah, actually. I'd better get out onto the platform in case I miss Professor Franzen."

So Penny, Vicky, Alastair and Spiky left the station restaurant. Because there were no trains arriving for a minute or two and therefore no desperate need for Vicky and Penny to seek out the particular platforms they each needed, the four of them stood together, chatting about the last time Spiky had been in Shrewsbury.

They were still deep in conversation as the Aberystwyth train came in. They were still deep in conversation as the passengers alighted. They were still deep in conversation as Alastair looked over his shoulder to see Beth, all lipstick and hair, marching towards them. She had not yet taken in the scene before her. Alastair said a silent prayer, hoping beyond hope that she would not stop and speak to him, that she would instead realise that he was with his wife and daughter, that she would therefore just keep walking, keep walking, keep walking.

Beth spotted the danger ahead of her, realising that Alastair was with his family. As she rushed past the Claytons, she accidentally brushed her suitcase against Penny's leg.

"Oh, I'm so very sorry," she said, alarmed that she had now brought attention to herself when that was the very last thing she had wanted.

"Oh, that's okay," said Penny, looking into the eyes of the glamorous younger woman. And then Penny recognised her as the stranger at the hospital, the one who had been loitering in the corridor that day, as if waiting for her moment. And then Penny knew in her heart that this lipsticked woman was surely also the one who had given her husband the GK Chesterton book and who had inscribed:

To my lovely Al,
Hope you enjoy this as you make a full recovery.
Love and kisses,
Beth
xxx

Penny remembered every word.
Beth, meanwhile, had rushed off toward the station exit.
"Don't you know that lady?" Penny asked her husband. And Beth, hearing the question as she sped away from the scene, quickly turned her head just in time to catch Alastair shaking his head dismissively and frowning as if to say: "Where on earth would I know *her* from?"

A minute passed in which no-one said anything.

Then Alastair glanced towards the exit. Beth had disappeared. His moment of anguish was over.

Penny and Alastair's attention was then taken by the expression on their daughter's face. She was looking beyond her parents towards a group of passengers now making their way down the platform from the Manchester train which had arrived as they were talking.

"What is it, darling?" asked Penny.

"Look," said Vicky.

Penny, Alastair and Spiky all looked to see a couple, arm in arm, swaggering towards them. It was Connor and a young woman.

"Did Connor know you were coming here tonight to meet him?" asked Penny.

"No. It was meant to be a surprise."

"Ah."

"Could be his sister," said Alastair, now relaxing somewhat, relieved that the evening had – for him, at least – not turned into the total disaster it could so easily have been.

"No matter how much a boy might love his sister, he would never hold her like that," said Vicky. "Furthermore, his sister is

Zoe, a very good friend of mine. That isn't Zoe."

And then the young couple stopped walking and kissed.

"Okay, it's not his sister," said Alastair.

As the couple approached, Connor noticed the Claytons. "Oh, hi you guys," he said. He quickly – and with obvious embarrassment – introduced the young lady he was with (she was called Sam and she was an old friend from Manchester). Connor exchanged a few awkward pleasantries with the Claytons and Spiky, and then headed, with his companion, for the exit.

"Ah, so the friend in Manchester wasn't so much a Sam, more a Samantha," said Vicky. "Not so much an old male school pal, but more like a sex goddess."

"What are you talking about?" asked Penelope.

"He's a liar, Mum. Connor is a bloody liar. He's been lying to me. He's even been lying to his sister. She was convinced the friend he kept going up to Manchester to see was a bloke. He's been stringing me along all this time, allowing me to believe that I might . . . oh, what the hell?" And a tear ran down her face.

"I'm sorry, Vick," said Penelope, offering her a tissue.

"He's not the boy we thought he was," said Alastair.

"It's the beauty thing again," said Vicky. "She's gorgeous. I'm not. I was never in his league."

"Hey, you listen to me, honeypie." It was Spiky Spencer eager to regain the initiative. "You've got it all wrong. A boy who doesn't care about upsetting a girl like you . . . well, if you ask me, it's him who's not in *your* league."

"Listen, Sweetheart. We'll have a good talk about this later – probably over a bottle of wine and a large box of chocolates," said Penny. "But why don't all you guys get off home now? I've got this Professor Franzen to meet, his train is due in in about ten minutes, and then we've got the Lit and Phil meeting, so I'll be home around eleven."

As Alastair, Vicky and Spiky made their way to the exit, Penny let go a huge sigh of relief. She felt that some higher power ought to be congratulating her on having looked that lipsticked woman in the eye without resorting to violence or, at the very least, verbal abuse. She felt she deserved some kind of medal for having behaved with such decorum and self-restraint.

But most of all, ten minutes later, as the man for whom she had been waiting, climbed down from the train, she congratulated herself for her on-the-spur-of-the-moment invention of a Professor Franzen, the expert on Dylan Thomas.

"Hello Penny," said the man.

She smiled, suddenly remembering long and exquisite summer afternoons of lying on the grass at the furthest faraway edge of the recreation grounds in Louth.

She flicked back her hair. "Hello Russ."

CHAPTER TEN

THE BELLE VUE TAVERN

A fortnight later...

Alastair was in the kitchen, trying to find the Penguin biscuits or KitKats that were usually kept in the bottom drawer. He pushed the roll of kitchen foil to one side in case they were underneath. He got down on his knees to get a better look.

"And what might you be looking for?" It was Penelope.

"Ah. I've been caught in the act," said Alastair.

"Try the pantry, my little chocoholic. I think I might have put them in there."

"Brilliant. Do you want one?"

"Is the Pope a Catholic?"

"And a cup of tea?"

"If you're making one."

"Well, I am, as a matter of fact."

They sat together in the lounge. It was a quiet Saturday afternoon.

"Look," said Penelope. "I really think it's time we had a

talk, my love. Don't you?"

"That sounds ominous."

"Not at all. I just feel we've been drifting for too long. Let's see if we can't do something to stop it."

"Drifting?" he asked. "As in drifting aimlessly?"

"No," she said. "As in drifting apart."

Alastair said nothing, but looked at his wife knowingly.

She continued: "While Vicky's out the house, let's have a conversation. I mean a real conversation. Let's see how that goes for starters. And if it goes well, who knows what might happen next?"

Alastair smiled.

Penelope snapped her KitKat in half and took a bite. She went across to the CD player and put on an Eva Cassidy album. It played softly and unobtrusively.

"Alastair, it's been a pretty awful few months. Ever since the car crash. I don't know if that has anything to do with it, really. It just seems that you've been different since the accident. Maybe I've been different too. We've not been as loving towards one another as we should have been. We've been, as I say, drifting . . . drifting slowly apart. I think now it's time we did something about it."

"I'm . . . I'm sorry, Penny, if I've . . ."

"Let me finish what I have to say first," she said softly. "This isn't about blame. This isn't about saying sorry. I think we've both been at fault. I want to try and build a bridge here."

Alastair nodded and took a sip of his tea.

"I'm not a fool," said Penny. "I know you've been keeping secrets from me."

Alastair almost choked on his tea, but remained silent.

"The girl – the woman, I should say – who came to visit you in hospital, the one who gave you the GK Chesterton book which you carelessly placed on your bedside table, the book with the inscription in it, the loving inscription. She was the woman on the railway station that night, wasn't she? The glamorous one. The lipsticked wonder. Very good-looking, I must admit."

"But Penny, my love, I . . . "

"Don't stop me. Let me have my say."

He put down his cup of tea and said quietly: "Right. I'll keep quiet then."

"You see, Alastair, I just want you to know that, yes, I am aware, or at least a little bit aware of what's been going on with you, but I also know that I am not completely blameless in this. We've both been keeping secrets. We've both been drifting away from this marriage."

And then Penelope suddenly began to wonder just how much she should say to her husband about her one meeting with her old flame on that evening when she and Alastair and their daughter had all bumped into each other on Shrewsbury Station.

She and her one-time long-ago boyfriend, Russ, had walked through the town to the Lion Hotel. As they had walked, they had talked passionately about their lives, about how things had turned out. They had laughed and they had enjoyed each other's company.

"It's wonderful to see you again after all this time," he had told her.

And at the Lion Hotel they had had a couple of drinks together, neither of them knowing where all this was going to end.

After the second drink, Russ had leant forward and kissed her. She had not resisted.

And, two hours later, two hours of talking but no more kissing later, on their slow walk back to the railway station, Penny and Russ had realised they would never see each other again.

She told him tenderly: "It's been a fantastic evening, Russ. It really has. But God alone knows just how many marriages have been broken up just by people – people like me – deciding on a whim to get in touch with some old flame through bloody social networking sites, and then one thing leading to another."

"Yes, I know. I know," he had said. "And you're right. It has been a fantastic evening."

Realising that actually Russ would be unlikely to begin a return journey to Lincolnshire that evening, Penny guessed he would probably find somewhere to spend the night in Shrewsbury, but she did not want to ask him about his arrangements. She knew that such a question might lead them somewhere else. And she assumed Russ was thinking the same thing because he did not broach the subject as they walked pointlessly back to the station.

Now Penelope pulled herself out of her reverie, looking her husband in the eye. "Aren't you going to finish your KitKat," she asked.

"You make it sound like a threat – *Finish your KitKat or I'll reveal yet more terrible secrets, ha, ha, ha!*"

And they smiled warmly at each other, the sort of looks they had not given each other in a very long time.

"I think perhaps, all I need to say now is this. I don't need to know about you and the lipsticked wonder. I don't need to know what happened or what didn't happen. I do know that I haven't been much of a wife these past few months. If you've been spending more time than you should down at the Belle Vue Tavern or else spending time lusting after other women, well, that's at least partially down to me not taking enough interest in you, not taking enough interest in us, not taking enough interest in our marriage. I want to change that, Alastair. I want to change that right now."

"Can I speak now?" he asked.

"If you like."

"I'm not going to lie to you, my love. I did have the hots for Beth – that's her name, the one you call the lipsticked wonder."

His wife laughed, but as she laughed a tear ran down her cheek.

"But you don't have to worry about any of that. We never got up to anything. We were only ever friends. Nothing more. And now she's found love through some online dating agency and she's got herself a new job and she's moving out of Shrewsbury so she can be nearer her new fella in Ludlow."

"That's nice to know," said Penelope, finding a tissue to wipe away the tear.

"Do you forgive me?" he asked.

"Do you need my forgiveness?"
"I think I do."
"Then I forgive you."
"Thank you," he said.

And then, screwing up his KitKat wrapper and popping it into the bin at the side of his armchair, he said: "Now, my love. Do you have any plans for the rest of the afternoon?"

Penny raised her eyebrows and said: "I do believe my diary is completely free."

Backhoe Billy was watching a football match on TV, a can of lager at his side. Although he tried hard to concentrate on the game, he could not help playing a scene over and over in his head; that damned kiss, that damned kiss between Vicky and Connor on stage that night. "No way that was acting," he told the television set. "No way."

He knocked back the last drop of lager and went off to the fridge to get another can.

"Jesus! Even football's not what is used to be," he said, returning to his chair.

The phone rang. For a second he wondered if it might be her.

It was a cold call.

Four days later, Vicky and her dad were sitting lazily, facing one another in a couple of armchairs in the lounge. Both were drinking from pint tankards. Both were drinking their favourite chilled Swedish pear cider. It was eight o'clock in the evening. Penny had gone to one of her Lit and Phil Society meetings. Chesterton was curled up and asleep at Vicky's feet.

"You know that gorgeous big bouquet that Billy sent you."
"That was ages ago, Dad."
"I know. I know. But let me finish. Did you ever respond to him in any way? Did you at least thank him for those flowers?"
"You know I didn't. We've been through all this before. Why do you keep dragging this up?"

"Because I think Billy is a smashing lad. And furthermore, and rather more importantly, I think you think he's a smashing lad too. I mean, what the hell was it that split you two up in the first place? You never did explain it to us. Which of course is your prerogative, but . . ."

"You really want to know?"

"I really want to know."

"It all came down to beauty."

"Beg your pardon?"

"I wasn't beautiful enough for him."

"Will you please stop talking in riddles and get to the damn point?"

"We were out together one night, walking back from the pictures. And he sees these two young girls on the other side of the street. Well, he could not take his eyes off them. Honest to God. He really could not take his eyes off them. I felt invisible. I felt hurt. I felt betrayed. I felt like a bloody idiot. And, perhaps worst of all, I felt unattractive. It's not a nice feeling when your boyfriend starts lusting after someone else."

"And what did Billy have to say about it?"

"Well of course he was very apologetic and all that. But I knew right there and then that I would never be as beautiful as the two girls on the other side of the street, and if it wasn't those two it would be the girl on the bus or the girl stepping out of the pub or the girl serving behind the counter at WH Smith's. I just knew that I couldn't compete."

"And you said all this to Billy at the time?"

"Yeah. More or less. I was angry."

"And he said?"

"That it didn't mean anything. That he cared about me and not the two girls on the other side of the street. But that didn't wash with me."

"Dya wanna know what I think, Vick?"

"I've no doubt you're going to tell me."

"Yeah. I *am* going to tell you. Because I'm your father and because I love you very much indeed and because, on this occasion, I think you've been rather silly and you need someone like me to point this out to you."

Vicky said nothing in reply, but took a sip from her drink and sat back in the armchair, as if to say 'carry on'

"Believe me, Vick. And I speak as a man. There is not a man alive, and there has not been a man since the dawn of time who hasn't fancied other women – women other than the wife, girlfriend, partner, whatever. It's only natural. You cannot just fancy one person and one person alone – that ain't gonna happen. And I would say it's exactly the same for ladies as well. They will sometimes take a liking to the postman or the milkman or some burly firefighter or someone on the telly – George Clooney or whoever. That does not mean that they don't love their husbands, boyfriends, partners, whatever. It just means they're human and occasionally another man will take their fancy. It's as simple as that. No harm in it. As my dad used to say, you can look but you can't touch."

Vicky smiled at her dad and said: "I suppose there might be something in what you say."

"Okay, now listen, sweetheart. You want my advice? Here it is. Connor didn't work out for you. He turned out to be a bit of a prat. Fair comment? I think so. Billy, on the other hand, cares for you. You said yourself he'd told you as much. I tend to believe him. He's a decent bloke. So this is what you do. You just give him a call. Tell him you took a bit of a wrong turning. Which people do from time to time. Because, when all is said and done, people are only human. You ask his forgiveness..."

"Er, sorry? Ask his forgiveness?"

"It doesn't do any harm to be a little humble sometimes. Yeah. Sure. Ask his forgiveness. He'll love that."

"Mmmm."

"And then – and here's the important bit – ask him out on a date."

Vicky beamed at her dad affectionately, said she had "a few things to do" and then went up to her room, taking her glass of pear cider with her.

Alastair idly ran his forefinger around the rim of his glass and thought again of that night at Shrewsbury Station, about how close he had been to meeting Beth and taking her out for the evening – a drink, a meal, who knows? And he thought about how his old friend Spiky Spencer had appeared from nowhere and turned things around.

It had turned out that Spiky had indeed, just as he had explained at the time, been on his way to a walking holiday, midweek to midweek. His connection at Shrewsbury had been delayed and he found himself with time to kill. Fate had then prompted him to head for the restaurant on the station to grab a coffee and something to eat, but then all his immediate plans had been abandoned once he had become embroiled in the Claytons' situation.

And Alastair, still sipping his pear cider, recalled now also how, later that strange night, he had asked Spiky just what had made him suddenly tell those lies to Penelope about him having texted ahead and about how he had arranged to meet up and go for a few pints . . . all that complete fabrication . . .

Alastair had asked his friend: "Where *did* all that come from? I mean, why did you think it necessary to lie like that on my behalf? How did you know I was in trouble?"

Spiky had told him: "Clayton, old buddy. You seem to forget. We go back a long way, you and I. All the way back to schooldays. All the way back to that day at the swimming baths when you started to go under. When I walked into the station restaurant that night, I saw the expression on your face. I'd seen that look on your face before. It was the look of someone drowning."

Upstairs in her room, Vicky played a Red Hot Chilli Peppers album, sipped her pear cider in communion with her father downstairs, and took from a drawer the letter Connor had sent her shortly after what he had described as "the unfortunate meeting" on the railway station.

For the umpteenth time, she read it:

My Dearest Vick,

I hardly know where to begin.

I suppose I must begin by saying sorry – the biggest sorry of my life. Never in a million years was it my intention to hurt you. I've been such a bloody fool.

Also, I want you to know that I really didn't mean to two-time you. Sam and I have known each other since our school days. We've been sort of sweet on each other since then. But then she went to live in Manchester and, although we've kept in touch right the way through, I'd pretty much given up on the two of us ever really getting it together.

I'd go up to Manchester every now and then and hang out with her. Sometimes she would come down and see me in Shrewsbury. But – romance-wise – it was never really going anywhere.

Over the years, she had a number of boyfriends and I was never anything more than a close friend.

Then – much to my surprise – there was a glimmer of hope (which sadly coincided with you and I meeting). And that's why I was always so very reluctant to turn our very good friendship (yours and mine) into anything more than that. Because I thought it wouldn't be fair to you. Because all the while, when we were going to Pigeons' rehearsals and all that, I thought there was a real chance now that Sam and I might finally get it together. Her letters and cards and emails to me had become more affectionate – romantic even. And although I was confused by it all, I couldn't help but wonder.

I knew you really liked me and wanted more from me, and I really fancied you too, but I was torn. I didn't want to build your hopes up if Sam, the love of my life, was just about to burst onto the scene in a big way.

Part of the reason, I think, why Sam and I were always at arm's length from one another was because I always imagined we would end up living in Shrewsbury together whereas, for years, Sam seemed settled in Manchester.

That all changed a little while ago when Sam saw a way of leaving Manchester and coming back to join me here.

"Yes, Connor," Vicky now told her dressing table. "Which is why you always asked your girlfriends if they loved

Shrewsbury . . . because you couldn't stand the notion of living anywhere else. I get that. So the moment your beloved Samantha said she could move back here, that was it. Perfect girl. Perfect location. Bingo!"

She picked up the letter again and continued reading:

I'm really, really, really sorry about the unfortunate meeting on the railway station. That must have been awful for you. It wasn't good for me either.

"It wasn't good for you either, you bastard!" said Vicky as the cat walked into her room. "Oh. I wasn't talking to you, Chesterton," she said.

She then screwed the letter into a ball and tossed it into her waste bin.

"I used to quite like your terrible jokes, Connor. But finally I realise that actually you yourself are just one big terrible joke. Good riddance!"

One week later . . .

It was the morning of Alastair's birthday. He went downstairs, put the kettle on and found a bowl for his Weetabix.

As he went to get the milk he noticed a message written in Early Learning Centre magnetic letters on the fridge:

I LOVE U

"Ahh," he said aloud to himself, and then went into the lounge to have his breakfast.

Penelope joined him there a few moments later, mug of coffee in hand.

"Have you seen what our daughter has put on the fridge for me?" he asked.

"Silly boy," said Penelope. "That wasn't Vicky who did

that."

"Oh," he said, and blew his wife a kiss.

That evening, Alastair, Penny and Vicky walked together down to the Belle Vue Tavern.

"This is nice," said Alastair, his wife taking his one arm, his daughter the other. He had no high expectations of the birthday celebration about to take place down at the local. A few great old records selected from the jukebox would do him, plus a few pints of beer, and the affection of his family.

That would be enough.

But – unbeknown to him – secret plans had been drawn up.

Alastair was surprised when the landlord wished him a happy birthday as he pulled the first pint of the night because although they knew each other a little, they did not know each other *that* well.

"Oh, you've been tipped off, have you? Well, cheers for that. Oh, and you've even got some live music on tonight in my honour," joked Alastair, spotting the microphone stand and speakers at the top end of the pub.

"You could say that," said the landlord.

Alastair laughed and went to sit down with his family.

Five minutes later, in walked John the retired baker, Paul the postman, and Frank the window cleaner, followed by Spiky Spencer and Alastair's mother-in-law Olivia.

"Okay, now this is getting a little spooky," said Alastair, getting up to greet them all. "I hope we're not putting you all up at our place tonight. We haven't got enough bedrooms for everyone."

"You can have your presents later," said Spiky. "But in the meantime, happy birthday, mate."

"Cheers, Buddy. Great to see you. Great to see you all. No, I mean it. I honestly wasn't expecting this."

He shook hands with each of his friends and gave his mother-in-law a hug.

"I have a feeling we could be in for quite an evening," said Alastair.

And then Backhoe Billy walked in. Vicky sprang to her feet and gave him a big hug and a kiss. She turned to her dad and said: "This one's with me. I gave him a call, Dad. Just like you suggested. We talked for an hour. I'll give you some money towards the phone bill. And, er . . . well. . . You'll be pleased to know, Dad . . . He forgave me."

Alastair shook Billy's hand and said: "And you, Mister. You're the icing on the cake. Brilliant to see you."

By now, a small crowd had gathered around the bar and most of the tables had been taken, making the pub busy and noisy and full of life.

"The surprises aren't over yet, Love," said Penelope. She walked up to the microphone stand.

"Blimey. She's not going to sing, is she?" asked Alastair.

"Ladies and gentleman," she began, "I have to tell you that, for some time now, my husband has been driving me mad by playing obscure folk-rock from the 1970s whenever we go on a long journey in the car. The band he has been playing on the CD player broke up decades ago. They were called Paper Bubble and they came from Shrewsbury. Well, with a little help from our daughter and through the magic of the internet, I was able to track down one of the main singer-songwriters from Paper Bubble, Mr Brian Crane, and I have very great pleasure in saying he is here tonight to play live for you, and especially for my birthday boy, Alastair."

"Oh, I don't believe it," said Alastair as Brian Crane stepped out from a shadowy corner, guitar in hand.

"Happy birthday, Alastair," said Brian, and then launched into the first song of the night.

As the spirit of the evening took hold, Olivia and Penny – the Denby girls – spoke excitedly of Olivia's plans to leave Lincolnshire and move to Shrewsbury; Vicky and Billy smooched in a corner; John, Frank and Paul teased Alastair about not having brought the Guardian with him tonight; and Spiky Spencer and Alastair made plans to go to the next Glastonbury Festival together, before they got too old for such things.

Asked how he was going to spend all the promised 'birthday money' that was coming his way from his wife, his daughter and his mother-in-law, Alastair replied: "You know what? Being the big kid that I am, I might just splash out on a model railway layout. Not a train set, you understand, but a proper model railway layout like the one my dad took me to see once — bridges, tunnels, a little village with a little pub and thatched cottages — the works."

Olivia, sipping a whisky and water, looked at her son-in-law fondly and said: "Alastair. I do believe — looking at that new-found sparkle in your eyes — that some of that good old non-specific spirituality is returning to you."

"Non-specific spirituality?" he asked.

"It's a phrase your wife once used in relation to you."

"'Magic' is a much snappier word," he said.

"Call it what you will, Alastair. But it's here tonight. That's for sure."

Two hours later, a few pints inside of him, Alastair picked up a beermat from the table. It had a slogan on it: "A pub is for life, not just for Christmas."

"That's us," he told Penelope.

"What?" she asked. "We're a pub?"

"You *know* what I mean."

"You're drunk," she said.

"I mean we are for life, not just for Christmas."

"Yes, dear." And she took his hand tenderly. And then she said quietly: "But you're still drunk."

Philip Gillam

ABOUT THE AUTHOR

Married with three sons, Philip Gillam is a journalist and author whose passions include pop music, the cinema, local history, the company of good friends, long walks in the country, and cosy pubs on winter nights.

He is the author of
Shrewsbury: A Celebration (Chasing Rainbows Publications, 2000),
Here Comes The Sun (UPSO, 2005)
and co-author – with Toby Neal – of
Shrewsbury: Pictures From The Past (Breedon Books, 2001),
Telford: Pictures From The Past (Breedon Books, 2002),
Shropshire: Pictures From The Past (Breedon Books, 2003).

As a journalist, Phil has interviewed pop stars including Ray Davies of The Kinks and Gilbert O'Sullivan, and major politicians including Tony Blair and Michael Heseltine. Feature writing assignments have seen him fly with the RAF in a jet fighter and go to sea with the RNLI.

He has worked for the Shrewsbury Chronicle,
the Sunday Independent, the Hull Times, the Staffordshire Newsletter,
the Stafford Chronicle, the Shropshire Star, and the Express & Star.
He is currently Editor of the Telford Journal and a columnist for the Shrewsbury Chronicle.

Twitter: https://twitter.com/SburyStation
Facebook: https://www.facebook.com/ShrewsburyStationJustAfterSix
Blog: http://shrewsburystationjustaftersix.blogspot.co.uk/

Printed in Poland
by Amazon Fulfillment
Poland Sp. z o.o., Wrocław